You are cordially invited

to the wedding of

Cole Dalton (who is not husband material)

and

??

Ceremony and reception coordinated by

Vivienne Shuster, who is definitely not

interested in the groom

\* \* \*

**MONTANA MAVERICKS**

Dear Reader,

I was so excited (and honored) when Harlequin asked me to write a book for the Montana Mavericks series. Then I was blown away when I found out that it would be about a wedding planner. I. LOVE. WEDDINGS. Big, small, traditional, unconventional...you name the type of wedding, and I am so there for it.

Writing *The Maverick's Bridal Bargain* brought back so many good (and nerve-racking) memories of planning my own ceremony and reception over fifteen years ago. As much as I loved my wedding, there are so many new ideas and trends and activities out there now that I sometimes wish I could do it all over again. Well, *most* of it over again. I could never beat our original vows—even though I cried when we were exchanging them.

Luckily, I got to relive the planning experience all over again with my latest heroine and expert event coordinator, Vivienne Shuster. When she and Cole Dalton, a best man with a hero complex, join forces to plan a fake wedding, they both get themselves into way more than they'd bargained for...

For more information on my other Harlequin Special Edition books, visit my website at christyjeffries.com, or chat with me on Twitter, @christyjeffries. You can also find me on Facebook and Instagram. I'd love to hear from you.

Enjoy,

*Christy Jeffries*

Facebook.com/authorchristyjeffries

Twitter.com/christyjeffries (@christyjeffries)

Instagram.com/christy_jeffries

# The Maverick's Bridal Bargain

*Christy Jeffries*

**HARLEQUIN® SPECIAL EDITION**

Special thanks and acknowledgment to Christy Jeffries for her contribution to the Montana Mavericks continuity.

Recycling programs
for this product may
not exist in your area.

ISBN-13: 978-1-335-46580-1

The Maverick's Bridal Bargain

Copyright © 2018 by Harlequin Books S.A.

**Printed in U.S.A.**

www.Harlequin.com

**Christy Jeffries** graduated from the University of California, Irvine, with a degree in criminology, and received her Juris Doctor from California Western School of Law. But drafting court documents and working in law enforcement was merely an apprenticeship for her current career in the dynamic field of mommyhood and romance writing. She lives in Southern California with her patient husband, two energetic sons and one sassy grandmother. Follow her online at christyjeffries.com.

### Books by Christy Jeffries

**Harlequin Special Edition**

***American Heroes***

*A Proposal for the Officer*

***Sugar Falls, Idaho***

*A Family Under the Stars*
*The Makeover Prescription*
*The Matchmaking Twins*
*From Dare to Due Date*
*Waking Up Wed*
*A Marine for His Mom*

Visit the Author Profile page at Harlequin.com.

To Stephanie Uribe Roman Phillips,
my college (and beyond) roommate,
my partner in crime, my wingwoman,
my dance floor equal, my V&T co-conspirator,
my maid of honor, my sister in mommyhood, my
therapist, my mainstay, my very best of best friends.
And that's just the first 25 years.

♥C

## *Chapter One*

While Vivienne Shuster no longer made assumptions about whose marriages would last, she could say with certainty that the bride and groom sitting across the conference-room table from her didn't appear to be the type who would maliciously smash cake in each other's faces.

Not that being a Junior Wedding Planner—yes, her boss had actually put that title on Vivienne's business cards—in Kalispell, Montana, gave Vivienne any sort of sneak peek into the future, but it did give her an inside track as to how a couple navigated one of the most stressful events of their relationship. Because if they couldn't deal well with simple decisions like color schemes and invite lists, the pair was doomed when it came to handling the more important realities of life after the wedding glow burned out.

Listening intently, Vivienne nodded as she scribbled notes inside the brand-new binder she'd started when Lydia Grant and Zach Dalton came into her office fifteen minutes ago. So far, Lydia was the ideal bride in that she was already eager to leave most of the details to Vivienne and seemed to be more excited over the prospect of getting married than the actual reception. In fact, the groom was the one who'd scheduled the initial consultation in an effort to take some of the pressure of planning off his soon-to-be wife.

Zach and Lydia were clearly enamored with each other and, so far, the meeting was going smoothly, with everyone on the same page. Vivienne wasn't surprised to find herself back on Team Romance—which was what she secretly called this euphoric mood that made her believe long-lasting love might actually be possible. It was times like these when she absolutely adored her job.

Unfortunately, in her chosen profession, the good moments were starting to become a lot less frequent than the headache-inducing ones.

Glancing at her slim smartwatch, she realized that she had only another hour before her boss showed up. Vivienne had purposely scheduled this appointment for seven in the morning, well before normal business hours, because she knew that her boss would be salivating once she found out that the couple wanted to have their wedding in Rust Creek Falls. The owner of Estelle's Events weighed all of ninety pounds—not counting her makeup and false eyelashes, which added at least another five—and had been smoking a pack a day for the past fifty years. If Estelle got her acrylic claws into this easygoing bride, then the small town of Rust Creek Falls, Montana, would never know what hit it.

"So we've got three bridesmaids," Vivienne confirmed with Lydia, before turning to Zach. "What about groomsmen?"

"Now, that may be a problem." Even without his Stetson, Zach was good-looking. But when the guy hitched up one side of his mouth into an aw-shucks grin, he became a double threat—gorgeous *and* charming. "I have four brothers."

"Four?" Vivienne gulped, blinking a few times to keep her eyes from bugging out. There was more than one handsome cowboy like this out there somewhere?

Zach pulled a picture from his wallet and handed it across the desk as though to prove it. She attempted to study the photo with as much professionalism as she could muster. There were two pairs of cowboys sitting on the top slat of a wooden corral, bookending a fifth cowboy who was standing in the middle. Zach was probably one of the sitters, but, honestly, Vivienne barely gave those guys a passing glance. She quickly narrowed in on the one in the center, though only because his central position and straight posture drew all of her attention. It had nothing to do with his sexy smirk or alert blue eyes. And it certainly wasn't because of the way his jeans fit perfectly on his—

"Is it a problem if we're uneven?" Lydia asked, yanking Vivienne out of her inappropriate thoughts. The bride-to-be was wearing jeans, a retro T-shirt advertising the band Lynyrd Skynyrd, and had a mess of brown curls piled into a ponytail. She definitely didn't strike Vivienne as the type to be bothered by unconventional appearances.

"No problem at all," she assured Lydia, smiling as she clung to the picture she wasn't quite ready to return. "It's your big day. There is no right way or wrong way to do things."

She snuck another peek at her watch, knowing the uproar Estelle would make if she overheard Vivienne saying that to a client. As a Junior Wedding Planner, Vivienne's so-called office actually doubled as the conference room and was currently open to the reception area so she could pull double duty as the receptionist. It also meant Vivienne could easily be overheard whenever she was talking to her clients, which was why she always tried to conduct these initial appointments when her boss wasn't around.

"So, with that many brothers, are you willing to pick just one to be the best man?" Vivienne asked, needing to move this meeting along but not wanting to rush Zach with what could be an important decision.

Judging by the happily casual way they were all posing in the picture, it was easy to make the assumption that the Dalton brothers were close. But as an only child, her experience in dealing with sibling rivalry had been limited to what she'd witnessed during prior weddings. She'd had her share of brides who didn't want a prettier sister upstaging them on their big day. There'd even once been an usher who decided that the start of his brother's ceremony would be the perfect time to propose to his own girlfriend. In short, nobody liked having their thunder stolen.

Zach held his cowboy hat in his lap, tapping the brim as he considered his options. Vivienne cleared her throat. "Or you could pick a friend or a cousin or even skip having a best man altogether."

He looked at Lydia, who simply shrugged. "It's up to you."

"I should go with Booker because he's the oldest," the groom began. "But Cole can have a bit of a hero complex and will think he's the only one—"

The front door creaked open, interrupting Zach and forcing all three of their heads to swivel down the short hall in that direction. Vivienne held her breath, praying it was only a delivery person and that Estelle hadn't decided to come in early.

But before she could stand up and intercept whoever it was, the middle cowboy from the picture strode across the reception area toward them, his boot heels clicking on the hardwood floor, his jeans well-worn and snug on his long, muscular legs. An electrical current shot through Vivienne and it took a few attempts for her to get her wobbly legs steady enough to rise to her feet.

How was it possible that the man was even better looking in person?

"Speak of the devil," Zach said to her and then also stood up and turned to the newcomer. "What are you doing here, Cole?"

"Did you even look at your left rear tire before driving all the way to Kalispell this morning?" the newcomer said to Zach. Then, as if suddenly realizing that his brother wasn't the only one in the room, the man removed his off-white cowboy hat and addressed his soon-to-be sister-in-law. "Hey, Lydia."

"Hi, Cole. This is our wedding planner, Vivienne Shuster," Lydia responded. "Vivienne, this is Cole Dalton, one of Zach's brothers."

Thankfully, Vivienne had braced one hand on the edge of the table when she leaned across it to shake his, because the warmth of Cole's palm enveloped her and she would've found herself moving in closer to him if there hadn't been three feet of heavily polished antique walnut separating them.

"Sorry to barge in on you like this, ma'am." His words drew her in even closer until her hips pressed against the table.

Growing up in Montana, despite having lived only in the bigger cities, Vivienne was accustomed to the occasional cowboy calling her *ma'am*. But there was something about Cole's voice that was both honey filled yet crisp at the same time. She cleared her throat and replied, "It's no problem."

"What's wrong with my left rear tire?" Zach's words penetrated Vivienne's improper fascination and, thankfully, reminded her to pull her hand back.

Her cheeks stung with heat as she looked down to straighten her still-empty binder, then took a swig of her iced coffee nearby. The last thing her overactive imagination needed was caffeine, but there were only so many things she could focus on besides the good-looking man with the sexy voice and mesmerizing handshake.

"When I went out to the stables this morning, I noticed the pressure was low," Cole told his brother, and Vivienne sank slowly into her chair, relieved that nobody else in the room was paying any attention to how her body had just responded to a complete stranger. "I was going to get the compressor out of the shed and fill it up for you after I got done changing the poultice on Zorro's foreleg. But you'd hightailed it out of there before I got back. Aunt Rita told me about your appointment, and the whole way here I had to keep my eyes peeled to make sure you weren't stranded on the side of the road with a flat."

Zach looked over his shoulder and mouthed the words *hero complex* to Vivienne and Lydia before turning back to his brother. "Why didn't you just call?"

"I did. You didn't answer. I also called the bridal shop here, but all I got was an answering service."

Vivienne was about to explain that they weren't just a bridal shop as well as the fact that, technically, they weren't open yet. But the concern on Cole's face seemed genuine, and his indignation about his brother's safety made the guy even more attractive, if that was possible.

Zach rolled his eyes, pulling his cell from his pocket. "Sorry, man. I must've accidentally set it on sleep mode."

"You know the family rule about phones." Cole crossed his arms over his broad chest, and his brother's expression turned from playful annoyance to humble remorse.

"You're right." Zach reached out and squeezed Cole's shoulder. "Why don't we go outside and look at my tire?"

The men excused themselves and the front door had

just clicked shut behind them when Vivienne asked Lydia, "What's the family rule about cell phones?"

She wanted to kick herself for asking a client such a personal question that was absolutely none of her business. But Lydia was an assistant manager and sort of reporter-at-large for a small-town newspaper and would, hopefully, understand Vivienne's blatant curiosity.

"Do you remember hearing about that horrible wildfire in Hardin last year?" At Vivienne's nod, Lydia continued. "Well, their ranch and the family house caught fire."

The woman looked up at the ceiling as though she was weighing whether or not to continue the story. When she lowered her head, Vivienne realized Lydia's eyes had grown damp. Reaching into her go bag, where she always kept an emergency stash of anything a bride might need on her big day, Vivienne grabbed a package of tissues and slid them across the table to Lydia. "That must've been a horrible loss."

"It was beyond horrible. Their mom was also in the house at the time and nobody had been able to warn her about the blaze because she'd left her cell phone in her car outside."

Vivienne's chest felt hollow and she pressed her lips together to keep from asking the obvious question. But judging by the way Lydia released a ragged breath, the answer was pretty clear. Her heart broke for Zach and Cole and, really, for all of the Dalton brothers. Especially since the loss of their mother was so recent.

She reached back into her go bag and replaced the tissues with a king-size bag of M&M's. Vivienne was no stranger to delicate situations, but some wedding dynamics called for a little more finesse and a lot more chocolate.

Cole Dalton didn't waste any time reading his brother the riot act as soon as their boots hit the parking lot. "Zach, it's one thing if you insist on driving around town on four bald tires when it's just you in the rig, but now that you're shackling yourself with a wife, you'll be responsible for someone else's safety and happiness."

"Shackling?" Zach lifted one of his eyebrows. "You make it sound like a prison sentence."

Cole sighed. "It's not that I think marriage is a prison sentence. After all, our parents were in love and probably would've been married for another thirty-five years…" He let his voice trail off. Nobody liked thinking about what could have been, and the men of the Dalton family especially weren't eager to talk about it. "Anyway, I'm sure you won't mess things up too badly with Lydia."

"Yeah, right. When you can commit to a woman for longer than a slow dance at the Ace in the Hole on a Saturday night, then you can give me relationship advice, big brother."

"Commit? Oh, please. I've got my hands so full looking out for you and the rest of our oversize family, I barely have time to schedule an appointment at the barbershop, let alone take a woman out on a proper date."

"Is that a fact?" Zach asked, and Cole took off his Stetson to show his brother how long it'd been since his last military-regulation haircut. Okay, so it had been only a few weeks, but when Cole had been on active duty in the Marine Corps, he was used to getting a high and tight every ten days. Zach whistled and replied, "It sure seemed like you had all the time in the world when you wouldn't let go of that pretty wedding planner's hand a few minutes ago."

Cole folded his arms over his chest, knowing his brother was just trying to rile him up. All the Dalton boys enjoyed going back and forth with each other like that. But the defensive stance also helped hide the way he was flexing his right hand, which still tingled from the softness of Vivienne's palm fitting so perfectly inside it.

Cole nodded toward the building's entrance. "I was just caught off guard by all the froufrou decorations in that war zone they call an office."

"War zone?" his brother repeated, his brow arched. "Froufrou?"

"It looked like someone crashed a Humvee full of roses into a lace factory. I mean, how many pictures of fancy white dresses and champagne glasses do they need in that place? It's like a single man's kryptonite inside of there, sucking out all masculine logic and rationale. You're lucky I was able to break you out when I did."

"I can't disagree with you on that, although I was surprised you were able to notice anything else in the room besides Vivienne." Zach grinned, then held up a hand when Cole began to argue. "As much as I'd love to stand out here in the parking lot and listen to you try to deny it, I need to go back inside, since I promised Lydia I wouldn't make her do all of this wedding planning alone."

"Fine. I'll take your truck over to the gas station up

the street and fill the tires while you finish." Cole held
out his palm and waited for Zach to toss him the keys.

"Thanks, man."

A few seconds later, Cole yelled across the parking lot to his brother's retreating back. "I'll leave them
under the floor mat when I'm done."

Because he sure as hell wasn't going back inside that
bridal shop and dealing with his unspotted attraction to some fancy—but totally unnecessary—wedding
planner. Cole shook his head as he hopped into the cab
of Zach's truck and started the engine. Some sappy love
song blasted out of the speakers and his finger dived toward the radio to switch off the country music station.

Yet he couldn't get the image of the blonde woman
out of his mind. Her hair had been pulled back into
some kind of loose ponytail, but he could tell it was
long and wavy and soft. Her white button-up shirt was
all business, and even her navy blue pin-striped skirt
was relatively professional, except for the fact that when
she'd stood up to greet him, she'd had to tug the hem
down. But not before he'd caught a glimpse of a dark
brown freckle on the inside of her thigh.

Her lips were soft and pink and her eyes were a fascinating shade of green. She was on the taller side, maybe
five-nine. He hadn't seen if she was wearing high heels
or not, but cool and classy ladies like that usually wore
fancy, useless shoes. However, all of those details were
slow to register with him because when he'd been shak-
ing her hand, Cole hadn't been able to think of anything
but that sexy little freckle.

He turned into the gas station and pulled the truck

up to the air hose before squeezing his eyes shut and trying to clear his head. It wasn't like Vivienne Shuster was the first good-looking woman Cole had ever met. He'd been in the Marines, stationed all over the United States, as well as a few bases overseas, and had always known where he could find a date on the few times he'd gone looking for a fun time.

So then why had his muscles gone all soft and his brain turned to mush when he'd met her?

Unlike his brother Zach, who'd actually placed an ad in the newspaper looking for a wife, relationships weren't exactly on Cole's radar at this juncture. Hell, they weren't even in his atmosphere.

Sure, once upon a time, he'd pictured himself moving back to Montana eventually and settling down with a wife and possibly having some kids of his own. But ever since his mom passed away, Cole had realized there were no absolutes in life. There was no point in planning that far into the future. Right now, his dad needed him. The property they'd been interested in buying fell through and, while they weren't exactly wearing out their welcome at the Circle D with his aunt and uncle, they still had to help their dad find a new ranch and get it running. Phil Dalton deserved to have a working place of his own, a place he could share with his sons. Yet Cole also owed it to his family to keep things as normal as possible, to prevent them from realizing how much responsibility he was shouldering.

So, yeah, he let his relatives think that he was in the market for the occasional date. He'd even gone out with a few women back when his cousin was filming that reality TV show in town. But Cole was always sure to flirt only with the ladies who didn't take him seriously. He certainly didn't react to them the way he'd responded to Vivienne.

But that was just a one-off. Surrounded by all that happily-ever-after propaganda and poster-sized images of wedded bliss back in her office—even for the few minutes he was exposed to it—who wouldn't have gotten overwhelmed and panicked? He'd been all fired up when he'd walked into her bridal shop, his worry and annoyance with Zach having snowballed during the twenty-minute drive there from Rust Creek Falls. Then, when he got inside, he was so out of his comfort zone he'd felt like one of those green plastic army toys thrown into a frilly, decked-out dollhouse. He'd had to do a complete one-eighty and rein himself in.

Cursing under his breath at his ridiculous reaction to the whole situation, Cole made quick work of the tires, using a pressure gauge he'd brought along with him to ensure that he didn't overinflate them. The sooner he returned the truck to the parking lot, the sooner he could get back to his aunt and uncle's ranch and let some much-needed manual labor push these fanciful notions from his mind.

Unfortunately, when he pulled into the parking lot of the tiny strip mall that housed Estelle's Events, his brother and Lydia were standing outside waiting for him.

Along with the wedding planner.

When Cole exited the truck, his eyes had a mind of their own and kept returning to that spot on Vivienne's skirt, hoping for another glimpse of her hidden freckle.

Since he couldn't very well pitch his brother's keys over the hood and beat a hasty retreat to his own truck, he was stuck with having to walk over to the trio. The smug grin on Zach's face reminded Cole of the time he'd lost a hay-bale-stacking race with his younger brother and had to volunteer to be on the prom committee at their small, rural high school. Although, the joke ended up being on Zach when Rondalee Franks—a senior on the cheerleading team who'd been in charge of decorating the gymnasium—asked Cole, a mere sophomore, to be her date. It wasn't his fault that the ladies loved a man who was always willing to help out.

The professional wedding planner, whose back was ramrod straight despite the uncomfortable-looking four-inch-high heels on her feet, had a death grip on a thick three-ring binder and didn't appear to be the type who needed assistance from anyone, let alone a former Marine-turned-rancher like him.

Cole knew that he should offer to shake Vivienne's hand goodbye, if only to prove to his brother—and himself—that his initial physical response to her was nothing out of the ordinary. Instead, he came only close enough to toss the keys to Zach. When a late-model purple Cadillac sedan pulled into the parking lot, he tipped his hat and simply said, "Ma'am."

Then he climbed into his own truck and refused to look back.

## Chapter Two

Vivienne's skin was still tingling from the sound of Cole Dalton's sexy drawl as she waved off Zach and Lydia before her boss got out of her car. Luckily, Estelle was still on the phone with one of their flower vendors when their newest clients drove away, saving Vivienne from an awkward introduction. Unfortunately, she hadn't been able to save them—or anyone else within a block radius—from hearing exactly what Estelle thought of having centerpieces set in burlap-covered mason jars, because the Cadillac's speaker volume was always set to Ridiculous.

Behind the windshield, Estelle's red acrylic fingernail jabbed toward Vivienne, the gesture clearly telling her that her boss wanted her to wait right where she was. After several minutes of threats to never refer another bride to them again, Estelle finally disconnected the call and exited the boatlike sedan like a ninety-pound bleached-blonde tornado, ready to blow through anything that stood in her way.

"Who was that leaving?" Estelle asked, not bothering to take off the giant tortoiseshell-framed sunglasses that hid more than half of her face, as well as the healing scars from her most recent visit to the plastic surgeon.

"Those are our new clients," Vivienne replied, her shoulders straighter than they had been for the past three months, when Estelle had first started pressuring her to bring in more bookings.

"Gah. More cowboy weddings," Estelle complained, before lighting up a cigarette. "I hope you told them that flannel isn't a bridesmaid dress option. We can't have people thinking we're running a rodeo over here."

"They're from Rust Creek Falls," Vivienne explained, waiting for the significance to sink in. Surely, the woman would be impressed now that their company was officially branching out into the small town that was becoming well-known for so many recent marriages.

"You got the full deposit from them, right?" The woman was happy only when money was exchanged. At Vivienne's nod, Estelle continued. "Good. Who was the other cowpoke with them?"

Despite the older woman's insulting tone, Vivienne's tummy did a somersault at the mention of Cole. "That's one of the groom's four brothers."

"Four?" Estelle pushed the supersize sunglasses on top of her teased platinum curls. Even the heavy mascara loaded onto her fake lashes couldn't conceal the gleam in her eye. "Are they all single?"

Vivienne flashed back to an earlier glimpse she'd had of Cole's strong, tanned fingers and reminded herself that the lack of a wedding ring didn't mean he wasn't in a serious relationship. "You know, I didn't think to ask."

"Well, find out if they are," Estelle told her, before reaching into the back seat. "Girl, in this business, you always need to be thinking one step ahead. If the other three are as good-looking as those two, there are bound to be some more weddings in the works. And I want *you* to book them."

A feeling of incompetence raced through her. They'd been having a similar conversation for the past year. She knew she was supposed to be bringing in more business, but there was something icky about force selling happily-ever-after. Vivienne was of the opinion that her work should speak for itself and happy couples would be more likely to refer their family and friends her way. But before she could argue as much, Estelle passed her a small plastic cage holding a shivering black-and-white guinea pig.

Their company had done weddings with everything from songbirds to butterfly releases to dogs as flower girls. But they'd never done one with rodents. Vivienne crinkled her nose. "What's this for?"

"When I went in for my post-op last week, the doctor told me my blood pressure has been through the roof lately. But with my high cholesterol and thyroid problems, I'm on so much stinkin' medication right now, the last thing I want to do is shove more pills

down my throat. Apparently, there've been recent stud-
ies about pets helping to ease people's stress levels, so
I thought I'd give it a try." Estelle used the remainder
of her cigarette to light up a new one before crushing
the butt under her size-four stiletto. Cutting back a
pack a day and not constantly yelling at wedding vendors would probably be more beneficial, but Vivienne
knew better than to suggest as much. "Since I'm al-
lergic to cats and I can't stand the stench of dogs, my
only choices at the pet shop were this little guy or a
turtle. And I don't do moldy tanks."

Vivienne held the cage up to eye level and peered
inside. There was something achingly familiar about
the startled fear reflected in the poor animal's eyes. "So
why did you bring him to the office?"

"The stupid thing is defective. It was up all night long
making this weird wheezing sound." Estelle grabbed
two binders off her back seat and hooked her trademark
purple tote bag over her bony shoulder. The ash from
her cigarette was almost an inch long and hanging on
precariously as she headed toward the office door. "I
need you to take him back to the pet store. Maybe you
can get me the turtle instead."

Vivienne was pretty sure the guinea pig wasn't defective; it was just overwhelmed. After all, Estelle's
nose and lungs had had decades to build up a tolerance
to her heavy-handed application of dime-store perfume
and her chain-smoking. Usually, Estelle never smoked
in front of clients, but since those had been scarcer
lately, her boss was lighting up at an alarming rate.

Vivienne remained outside in the parking lot, setting

the cheap plastic cage on the hood of Estelle's car. She wanted to unlatch the metal door, but she was afraid the thing would run away.

"What am I going to do with you?" she asked. The guinea pig twitched its nose in response, the whiskers on either side of its face quivering.

Vivienne wasn't much of an animal person. Growing up, she'd had only one pet, and that had been short-lived. When her parents divorced the first time, not only had they fought for custody of Vivienne, they'd also fought for custody of Filmore, a fluffy Pomeranian who didn't understand the concept of every-other-week visitation. Vivienne was at school one day when Filmore snuck out of her dad's sparsely furnished apartment and tried to make his way back to the house he was used to—the split-level home her mom got in the divorce. He never made it.

Her mother accused her father of giving the dog to one of his girlfriends, and her father accused her mother of leaving a trail of bacon the entire two miles between his apartment and her house. At first, Vivienne was heartbroken over her lost pet, but a week later, she was getting off the school bus a block away from her mom's place and saw Filmore in the window of the Petersons' house. She knew the Peterson girls from school. They were younger, and their parents never screamed at each other on the front lawn like hers did. So Vivienne decided not to say anything, because at least Filmore would get to live with a happy family even if she couldn't. Every once in a while, she would go over to their house and pretend she was interested in having make-believe tea parties and playing with their babyish pink palace dream house just so that she could visit her dog.

When her mom and dad eventually got back together, Vivienne asked if they could go over to the Petersons' and get Filmore. However, her parents were so caught up in each other and making up for lost time that they didn't want the burden of a pet again.

Vivienne bit her lower lip as she studied the helpless guinea pig. Maybe she should take him back to her apartment for now. She should also call the pet store and tell them that under no circumstances were they to sell that poor turtle to Estelle. But, first, she had a wedding to put together. Balancing her binder in one arm, she carried the cage into the office.

The peanut M&M's were long gone, so she broke off a piece of the granola bar she'd thrown in her purse this morning when she realized she wouldn't have time for breakfast, then pushed it through one of the slots toward her new friend. The guinea pig cautiously moved forward and sniffed the food before using its tiny paws to shove the whole thing into its cheek. Then Vivienne settled into her chair and got to work.

She opened the binder to see that a photo had gotten stuck inside one of the divider pockets. And not just any photo. *The* photo. All five of the Dalton brothers were handsome. And after hearing about the tragedy of losing their mother, Vivienne was fascinated to find out more about them. She told herself she was interested in learning all their stories, but it was really Cole she stared at, Cole's story she wanted to hear.

Something inside of her ached. Maybe it was all the romance novels and bridal magazines pulling at her heartstrings. She'd read her fair share of both, and every once in a while she could forget about the bridezillas and the uninterested grooms and the wedding marketing ploys and wonder if there was such a thing as love at first sight.

Not for her, of course. Having witnessed the whirlwind of her parents' marriage, Vivienne was smart enough to want to get to know her future husband for at least a few years before she decided if they were compatible.

She was also smart enough not to get all worked up by a pair of well-worn jeans and a sexy smirk and a honeyed voice calling her *ma'am*.

A week later at the Circle D, Cole was in one of the corrals exercising his uncle's injured horse when a Jetta zipped down the driveway toward the ranch house. As the car approached, he recognized Vivienne behind the wheel and his pulse sped up. Paying attention to the driver instead of where he was going, Cole kept walking straight as the horse rounded the turn. Zorro's front hoof grazed the side of his boot, causing them both to stumble.

"Easy, boy," he said more to himself than to the stallion.

She was wearing some sort of silky floral dress that wrapped around her curves like a second skin, and her high heels had no business navigating the dirt driveway, which was still fairly muddy after a recent spring rain. Balancing that big binder on her hip, Vivienne used her free hand to carry a tall vase. A strong wind caused the side of her dress to flip open and his lungs froze as he was treated to a full view of her shapely thighs. When she tried to pull her dress back into place, she dropped the binder, its contents spilling out everywhere.

Quickly, Cole secured the lead rope to the mechanical arm of the hot-walker, then hopped over the fence, mentally kicking himself for initially staring at her like a lovesick calf instead of immediately rushing to her aid. On his way, he picked up scattered papers and pictures of cakes and flowers. The dainty images and carefully handwritten lists made his work-roughened hands look big and coarse, and he quickly shoved the stack at her.

"Thank you," she said, not noticing that the notebook she'd just pulled to her chest was covered with mud. "I'm supposed to meet Zach and Lydia here at the ranch and then drive over to check out Maverick Manor as an option for a wedding venue. But I'm running a little early."

"You're getting dirt all over your..." He pointed at the mud now covering the neckline of her dress, then slammed his fingers into his front pockets when he realized he was gesturing toward her breasts. When she pulled the binder closer as if she could shield his inappropriate gaze, he felt his cheeks flame.

"Do you want to wait for them on the porch?" he asked. He had no idea when Zach and Lydia would get here, and while Cole could rescue windblown papers, he wasn't much for entertaining guests or making small talk. Racking his brain, he asked himself what his aunt Rita would do if she were home. "Can I get you a drink?"

Vivienne rotated her slender wrist to glance at her watch. "Actually, if you wouldn't mind me using the restroom, I could try to clean myself up a little before they get here."

"No problem," he said, taking the tall vase from her. "Follow me."

He slowed his pace so that she could better follow him without getting one of her heels stuck in the driveway. His uncle and aunt's sprawling log ranch house was pretty big, but with Cole's dad and brothers living there temporarily, he couldn't vouch for the cleanliness of anyone else's bathroom but his own.

He said as much as he led her down the hallway toward the girls' wing. Then, because he didn't want her getting the wrong idea about where he was taking her, he added, "We have to walk through here to get to the Jack-and-Jill-style bathroom."

"This is *your* bedroom?" she asked, her gaze focused on the fierce pink sign on the door ordering all boys to keep out.

"Originally, the two rooms on this side of the house belonged to my cousins Kristen and Kayla before they got married. So I can't take credit for the decor. All the frills and ruffles and throw pillows were here when I moved in."

"That's good to know." Vivienne's playful smile sent an electrical current through his gut. "I had you pegged for more of a roses-and-chintz type of guy, so the daisy quilt and eyelet curtains threw me off for a second."

"Roses? Me? And here I thought I was sending out a strong tulip vibe." He grinned back at her and then continued on toward the bathroom.

"I think it's sweet that your masculinity isn't threatened by a few pastels and floral prints."

"Listen, I slept in much worse conditions when I was deployed in the Marine Corps."

She didn't respond, so he turned back to see if she was still following him. Vivienne had paused right outside the bathroom door, her head tilted. "You were in the Marines?"

"You seem surprised," Cole replied.

"In my line of work, I try to never be too surprised about anyone." She crossed over the threshold and set her muddy binder down on the tile counter. "Although, I had assumed that you were just a cowboy."

"*Just* a cowboy?"

"I didn't mean it like that. I meant like a full-time job. Your brother Zach mentioned that he's been so busy working here with your uncle and helping your father find a new ranch. I saw the picture of you with your brothers dressed up in—" she gestured toward his daily uniform of boots, jeans and a flannel shirt "—all that cowboy gear and I figured that you guys all worked together."

"Some of us work harder than others," he said as he winked. Then he wanted to kick himself for flirting when nobody was even around to witness it. Well, nobody except Vivienne, who seemed way too serious and professional to engage in harmless bantering. Still, she had made the first joke, so maybe he'd read her wrong. "If it's any consolation, you were right and I'm now a full-time cowboy."

"So then you're not a Marine anymore?"

"Well, you know what they say. Once a Marine, always a Marine." He saw the confusion creasing the smooth skin of her forehead. "I put in my time and was honorably discharged."

"Oh. How long did you serve?" Vivienne focused on him when almost any woman he knew would've already directed her full attention to her own reflection in the nearby mirror, worrying how she would get all that dirt off her pretty dress.

Cole was surprised by how natural it would've felt to hitch his hip up onto the countertop and shoot the breeze with her. Five minutes ago, he'd been dreading talking to her about anything more substantial than whether she preferred ice in her sweet tea. Yet the lady who had at first appeared to be all business now seemed completely at ease making small talk in such close and personal quarters.

Unfortunately, his departure from the Corps and the circumstances surrounding it brought back the painful memory he would never be comfortable talking about with anyone, let alone a stranger—no matter how attractive she was.

Instead, he did what he always did when he wanted to avoid something. He winked and made a wisecrack. "You'd need to have security clearance to get that type of information out of me."

Vivienne's hand rested casually on the edge of the sink as she faced him and wiggled her eyebrows. "As the wedding planner, you'd be amazed at some of the insider intel I can access."

His glance dipped down to the V of her dress as he considered how far she might go in her fact-finding mission. A throbbing of awareness below his belt buckle yanked him back to reality. When he dragged his eyes up to meet hers, she was staring at him in a way that made him feel completely exposed.

Cole purposely broke eye contact by reaching for a couple of pink washcloths in the cabinet before handing one to her. "Why's that?"

"In addition to organizing everything, my job is to be part psychologist, part coach, part fortune teller and a full-time mediator. I have to get all the data I can about not only the couple, but also their friends and their families, to prepare for a multitude of possibilities."

"But it's just a wedding. What could possibly go wrong?" he asked as he began cleaning the binder in one of the bathroom sinks.

She used a washcloth at the other sink to wipe the spot of mud on her dress, looking in the mirror as she spoke. "I need to know which uncle—or aunt—is likely to have too much to drink. I have to make sure that there aren't any bickering cousins sitting together at the head table or any exes coming as someone else's plus-one. It helps to find out in advance if the father of the bride has any food allergies and what the mother of the groom's favorite song is for the..." Regret dawned in her eyes and, thankfully, she caught herself just before saying the words *mother and son dance*.

But the image was already out there for Cole.

His mom.

The woman who'd dreamed of being a dancer on Broadway before she'd fallen in love with a rancher from Montana. The woman who'd taught them all how to do a basic waltz and an electric slide before they were in sixth grade. The woman who used to stop whatever she was doing when the perfect two-stepping beat came on the radio, grab whichever boy was nearest to her and then laugh and sing as she twirled a kid around the house.

Diana Dalton would never get to dance at any of her sons' weddings. The thought was like a punch to Cole's gut.

"I am so sorry," Vivienne began, but he held up a palm. Hearing her pity would only make the guilt twist deeper inside of him.

"Don't worry about it." He forced his tense lips into a casual smile, but his reflection revealed that it was more of an uncomfortable grimace. They were looking at each other through the mirror, and even though it wasn't direct eye contact, it was still too much. He grabbed a towel off the rack behind him, buying himself a few seconds to regain his composure before he turned back.

Vivienne's own hands had stilled under the stream, so he shut off the water and passed her the clean binder. His voice sounded normal enough when he said, "Here. Good as new."

Then he reached for another brightly colored hand towel and held it out to her. She opened her mouth, but before she could apologize, he cut her off. "Don't tell my brothers this, but when we moved to the Circle D, I purposely drew the short straw because I've always been partial to the color pink anyway."

Then, as if to prove that everything was fine, he gave her another wink in the mirror before walking out.

## Chapter Three

Vivienne lingered in the bathroom a few more minutes, mentally berating herself for slipping like that and bringing up Cole's mother. Bracing her hands on the counter, she bent her head and tried to reason that she hadn't technically been referring to *his* mother. Still, the angst that had flashed across his face was due to a freshly painful subject that she'd brought up.

She pinched her eyes shut. Vivienne was usually much more sensitive in her dealings with clients, even if they looked like ruggedly tough cowboys who were quick to tease. But she hadn't been herself since the moment she'd driven up. When she'd gotten out of her car earlier, she'd been surprised to see Cole outside, his shirtsleeves rolled up and working with that horse like a hero out of some Western novel. Something had stirred inside of her and she'd tried to distract herself with the task of getting too many things out of her trunk at once.

Then she'd accidentally flashed him when her wrap-around skirt had blown apart, and she'd dropped everything she'd brought, including her pride. She'd been speechless and muddy and completely vulnerable, which must've been the reason she'd willingly followed the man into his bedroom of all places.

It had taken every last bit of nerve she possessed to look Cole in the eye and make small talk with him as though having conversations with strange men in the tight confines of their bathrooms was the most normal thing in the world. Vivienne had been forced to focus on his face so that her eyes wouldn't dart off and stare at the shower just behind where he'd been standing. She had done her best to maintain an ounce of professionalism while simultaneously imagining what he would look like all damp and steamy, wrapped in nothing but the small towel hanging on the hook beside the beveled-glass-door shower stall.

They had been inches apart at side-by-side sinks for goodness' sakes! Was there ever a more intimate environment to be in with a man? How would she know? The few relationships she'd had in college were with guys who lived in different dorms, and she'd never seen a need to sleep over. After graduation, she'd made her job her top priority and had gone on only a handful of dates since then—none of which required the sharing of a bathroom.

Vivienne looked back at the boy-band poster taped to the wall behind her. Okay, so maybe this particular bathroom wasn't *that* intimate of an environment. But Cole had been wearing those jeans and doing that lazy smirk, and her brain had gone all cloudy. Obviously, she hadn't been in her right mind or else she never would have mentioned mothers at all.

Sure, he'd bounced back from her inept comment fairly quickly, graciously acting like nothing was wrong. He'd even delivered a saucy wink that was so believable she'd all but dropped her stupid binder a second time on the ivory-and-pink rag rug.

Vivienne frowned at the binder. She preferred to keep most of her work on an electronic tablet, but Estelle insisted on having hard copies of everything. The three-ring notebook made her feel as though she was back in middle school, a trusty Trapper Keeper in her arms the only thing separating her from the cute boy who had the locker right next to hers.

It also made her feel as though she was constantly lugging her boss around with her, a not-so-subtle reminder that she was supposed to be booking more clients. Not only did she need to be professional and do her job, she needed to do it well enough that others would be willing to hire her, as well. And flirting with the groom's brother in the bathroom was not the way to accomplish her career goals.

Standing up straighter, she decided that she'd already hidden out in Cole's bathroom long enough. Plus, she was pretty sure she heard voices coming from somewhere outside, so it was time to get to work.

Vivienne wished she had paid more attention to the house layout when she'd followed Cole back here. Instead, she'd kept staring at his jeans-clad rear end, and now she was stuck navigating her way back to the main area of the house. She made only one wrong turn, telling herself that every framed family photo on the wall was merely insight to better understanding her clients.

Relief flooded through her when she spotted Lydia and Zach in the front room. Thankfully, there was no sign of Cole.

"Sorry we're late," Lydia said.

Vivienne waved her off. "No, I was early."

The three of them stood there for a few awkward moments until Vivienne finally asked, "Should we sit down somewhere?"

"Sorry," Zach said, somewhat sheepishly. "I may be living here, but I'm not used to playing host. Why don't we head over to the kitchen table?"

Vivienne followed the couple into the large, sunny kitchen and came up short when she saw Cole standing in front of the refrigerator with a big plate covered in foil. "Don't mind me," he told them. "I worked through lunch and wanted to grab a quick snack."

"Does Aunt Rita have any of that lemon icebox pie left over from last night?" Zach asked his brother.

"She did," Cole replied, before hiding the plate behind his back. "Finders keepers."

Zach responded with a noise that sounded suspiciously like an oink, then lunged at his brother's elbow, trying to pull his arm forward.

"I'm the pig?" Cole used his shoulder to deliver a powerful block. "Don't you have a fancy tuxedo you're gonna need to fit into?"

"Do I have to wear a tux?" Zach turned toward her and Lydia, causing Vivienne to let out the breath she'd been holding when she thought the two brothers were going to come to blows over a piece of dessert.

Lydia looked at her for the answer. Vivienne cleared her throat. "Not if you don't want to. You can dress as formally or as casually as you like. But since we're talking about outfits, have you guys thought about a color scheme?"

Vivienne opened the binder on the table and pulled out several pictures she'd printed after the first meeting with the couple. They spoke about suits and lace and blush pink and everything Vivienne easily discussed on any given day. However, her mind was completely elsewhere, and she found herself constantly losing her train of thought.

Cole opened cupboard doors and shuffled things around inside the fridge as though he were scavenging for more food. Yet he didn't eat another bite. His mouth was too busy sputtering anytime Vivienne answered a question or made a suggestion. It was obvious he was not only listening to every word they were saying, but that he also had a completely differing set of opinions.

After Cole had snorted for at least the seventh time, Zach finally said, "Please ignore my brother. He thinks he's an expert on everything, including event planning, apparently."

"Pfshh. I'm an expert on not wanting to go to lame events."

"Lame?" Zach repeated. "Back in high school, his idea of a party was to invite all of his junior lifeguarding buddies from the community pool over to our house for a refresher course in CPR."

Cole's eyes narrowed as his lips eased into another one of those slow smirks. "Maybe we just wanted an excuse to practice mouth-to-mouth resuscitation on some pretty teenage girls."

"Yeah, right." Zach chuckled before cupping his hand around his mouth to stage-whisper, "Shawn and I were spying on them and the only exchanging of saliva came when Rondalee Franks double-dipped her carrots in the ranch dressing. And even that was limited, since Cole launched himself at the dip bowl like it was a live grenade."

"What can I say?" Cole shrugged. "I saved everyone from a potential outbreak of mononucleosis."

"That's right." Zach pointed a finger at his brother. "Wasn't she the girl who was absent from school for a couple of months?"

"Yes. And you're welcome." Cole made an exaggerated bow and Zach threw the crumpled-up piece of foil from the pie plate at him.

"If you really wanted to be useful, you could whip up a plate of brownies or at least set out some cheese and crackers for our guests."

"For Lydia and Vivienne, I might be willing to rustle up something," Cole said as he pulled a bag of potato chips out of the pantry. "But you should probably lay off the carbs if you plan to hire a professional photographer. I hear the camera adds ten pounds."

Both Dalton men were six feet tall, with similar lean, muscular builds. While Vivienne was more appreciative of the way Cole filled out his jeans, neither one was at risk of needing to watch his calories. But that didn't stop them from arguing over who was entitled to which snack.

Someone needed to pass Vivienne something to eat soon, because she couldn't keep up this charade for long. Stress made her hungry, and while this was one of the easiest couples to work with, Cole's constant presence wasn't exactly relaxing, despite her comfortable seat at the long pine table. If the awkward moment in the bathroom hadn't happened, she might be able to enjoy this family's teasing camaraderie. But that wasn't what she was getting paid to do.

"All this talk about food brings up another thing we need to be thinking about before we go look at venues," Vivienne said in an effort to smoothly transition the conversation back to the purpose of their meeting. "Do you guys have a preference for a buffet, or would you rather serve a formal plated meal?"

"Hmm. I guess we have to feed our guests, don't we?" Lydia put her elbow on the table and propped her chin on her hand.

"Not necessarily." Vivienne gave a discreet cough, attempting to block out Estelle's voice in her head drilling her to always upsell. "Some couples prefer to save money by having only light refreshments and cake."

Luckily, this particular bride and groom had already laid out their budget at the initial meeting, and she doubted that Zach and Lydia would be the type to skimp on their guests' comfort. Still, she felt the need to always give people their options.

"Seems to me like you guys should just drive over to the courthouse, say the I do's and be done with the whole thing." Cole gestured at the binder. "That paper you guys sign is going to be the same whether you throw away all your money on this nonsense or not."

Nonsense? Did the man realize that he was indirectly implying that Vivienne and her job were completely useless, as well? Her spine straightened at the insult but soon lost some of its steel resolve when she couldn't really argue the point. More often than not, she felt that weddings and even marriages were just a big waste of effort and time. But she wasn't about to admit as much in front of her clients. She was supposed to be drumming up more business, not losing it.

Thankfully, Lydia jumped in. "Cole, this wedding isn't just about me and Zach. It's about our families and our friends and our journey to finding each other. It may be nonsense to you, but to me, it's an opportunity to celebrate everything and everyone who is important in our relationship."

Zach opened his mouth—probably to defend his bride, who was clearly capable of speaking up for herself—but his cell phone went off at the exact same time Cole pulled his own vibrating phone from his pocket.

"It's a group text from Dad," Cole said first.

"I know," Zach replied, not looking up from his cell. "I'm part of the group."

It seemed like a race to see which brother could read the message first. Not that she had a view of anyone's screens from her seat on the opposite side of the table, but curiosity had Vivienne scooting closer to the edge of her chair.

Cole's fingers were already flying across the electronic keyboard, likely because he wanted to be the first to respond. She was sensing a competitive edge to the middle Dalton son.

Luckily, Zach didn't appear to have the same sense of urgency to reply, because he announced, "Looks like Dad just made an offer on some property a few miles away."

"That's fantastic," Lydia said. "Where is it?"

"He said Sawmill Station," Zach replied. "I know we're still pretty new to Rust Creek and I've heard of Sawmill Road. But I've never heard of a ranch by that name."

Lydia tilted her head. "That's because Sawmill Station isn't a ranch. It's an old abandoned train depot."

"Why would Dad make an offer on an abandoned train depot?" Cole asked as he continued typing.

Zach's phone made another ping. "I'd ask him, but I can't dial out when my phone keeps buzzing with incoming texts from you."

"I just told him that I'm here at the Circle D with you and we can swing by to check it out."

"I know," Zach told his brother, holding up his phone. "I can read."

Lydia looked at her watch. "We have another hour before our appointment at Maverick Manor in town. Since Sawmill Station is on the way, we could swing by and check it out. Would you mind, Vivienne?"

She leaned back slowly in her chair to prevent herself from sliding under the table to get away from Cole's penetrating stare. Anticipation hummed through the kitchen and it was obvious that buying this property was a monumental occasion for the Dalton family. Normally, she liked to meet with her clients at their homes or workplaces because seeing them in their natural surroundings gave her a better sense of their personalities, which translated to a fuller picture of how they envisioned their big day. However, tagging along on a private family outing was surely beyond the boundaries of her job description.

Yet all three of them looked so eager she couldn't very well deny them their side trip. And they could just as easily discuss bouquets and music playlists in the car. Besides, this was her last appointment of the day. The only thing waiting for her at home was a to-go box containing half of a three-day-old club sandwich, and an unsocial guinea pig who refused to come out of its cage.

Vivienne managed a weak smile and said, "Sure. Why not?"

Cole should've just driven his own truck, but GPS navigational systems were still spotty this far out and Lydia was the only person who knew exactly where they were going. They could've gone caravan style, but Cole had never been the type to blindly follow while one of his brothers took the lead. Riding together seemed like the most logical solution.

Of course, that was before he realized that he'd be crammed into the back seat of the crew cab next to the hoity-toity wedding planner who kept her body so stiff there wasn't a bump or pothole along the way that would dislodge her from her seat-belted perch.

Fortunately, the soft fabric of her overlapping skirt wasn't as rigid and would gape open a little wider every time his brother navigated a curve on the winding, narrow road that led to the new property. Cole had just gotten a peek of the freckle on Vivienne's thigh when the truck made a sharp right at a faded yellow sign that might've once read Sawmill Station.

"I thought Dad was going to buy an actual ranch," Zach commented as he slowed the vehicle in front of a run-down brick building that was way too enormous to be a barn or a stable.

"It's certainly a far cry from the Circle D," Cole agreed. "But Dad said he was buying it for the acreage. I guess we're supposed to envision it once we get those old structures torn down and some pastures mapped out."

Lydia's yelp from the front seat was more like a squeak. "You can't just tear down those buildings. They're historical landmarks."

Cole waited for Zach to put the truck in Park before unbuckling his seat belt. As he hopped out, he asked, "Are we going to run a ranch or a museum?"

He walked around to the passenger side of the truck, where Vivienne was tentatively placing one high-heeled foot on the running board in order to climb down. Cole reached out instinctively and cupped her elbow as she descended onto the mud-caked asphalt. Feeling a tug low in his belly at her nearness, he had to force himself to let go when she began to straighten her skirt.

"I recently helped out on an article about all the

abandoned railway lines in Montana," Lydia said with some awe as the four of them stood in a row in the weed-infested gravel driveway. "A hundred or so years ago, this property used to be a feed mill and ran adjacent to a logging camp. Back then, the best way for businesses to distribute their products throughout the West was by freight car. The original owners laid some tracks and opened a small depot, naming the place Sawmill Station. Their vision was shortsighted, though, because, as you know, the logging industry never stayed in one place very long, so the camp moved on. Then as more ranchers came out west, the feed mill's business boomed. Unfortunately, this location was pretty remote, and with the invention of eighteen-wheelers and interstates, using trains way out here fell by the wayside. The company had to change with the times and eventually relocated to Kalispell."

Cole had always thought himself to be too practical for nostalgia, but the acreage was vast and grassy if he looked past the buildings. Plus, it was kind of cool to own a place with a little bit of history, a place that someone else had once sunk their own blood and sweat into. Maybe it was all those years living in barracks on military bases, but he was itching to replant some roots and this neglected-looking property needed him. It felt good to be needed again.

The possibility of a challenge flared up inside of him and he wondered out loud, "So maybe instead of bulldozing everything to the ground, we can repurpose some of these buildings. If only we knew what was what."

"Down at the *Gazette* offices, I think we have an old photo of this place in its heyday," Lydia explained, walking toward a smaller structure. "I believe that this peeling white building up front is the actual depot, but because nobody in town came this far out, it never saw too many passengers. That huge brick monstrosity back there is a freight house, where they'd store the loaded cars."

"Looks like they left one behind when they closed down operations." Vivienne pointed to an abandoned railcar sitting at a crooked angle, the lower half almost hidden by overgrown grass and the inside probably home to several different species of critters. Cole watched the wedding planner as she studied their surroundings. He'd half expected her to jump back into the truck at the first sight of a prairie dog. But she surprised him when she said, "There's something alluring and fascinating about it all, isn't there? I mean, all that rustic brick is totally back in style right now. And the tiny depot is adorable. Can't you just picture what it would look like with a fresh coat of white paint and some flower boxes planted around the platform?"

"What *used* to be the platform, you mean." Cole squinted at the collapsed, rotted-out planks.

"Let's go check out the freight house," Vivienne suggested, surprising him again by leading the way. Her legs trembled slightly as she trudged through the path in her high heels, and Cole found himself appreciating her determination and curiosity.

When they got to the wooden plank doors of the large brick structure, he saw that the padlock was relatively new, but the hasp was so rusted that it all but fell at Zach's feet when his brother gave it a slight tug.

"Whoa," Cole said, taking a step back. "Isn't that breaking and entering?"

"Not if you guys own the property," Vivienne replied, before being the first to walk inside. Cole almost asked if prowling and trespassing were included in her wedding-planner fees, or if she charged extra for that service.

"We don't own it yet," Cole called out when Zach and Lydia followed her lead. Super. Now they were all committing a crime. He stepped in after them. "Technically, Dad never mentioned whether or not the offer was accepted."

"Relax, Sergeant Save-the-Day," Zach said, using the hated nickname from childhood. "The lock is probably just to keep out the bears and the teenagers looking for a hangout. It's not like they're storing any valuables in here."

Okay, so maybe his brother had a point. Aside from some spiderwebs and a few broken wooden crates in one corner, the place was empty.

"Wow." Vivienne did a complete circle as she looked up at the row of dormer windows lining each side of the roofline. "Look at all the natural light coming in here. An open floor plan like this would be the perfect place to host some sort of housewarming party."

Cole squeezed his eyelids shut for a few seconds, then opened them, wondering if the woman was seeing the same run-down barren building he was. Who in their right mind would throw a party here? Or maybe the fee calculator in her mind was ka-chinging like a cash register, and Vivienne was hoping to make a killing on his family with her suggestions for additional parties they didn't need.

"I'm afraid your vision is completely lost on me," he said, crossing his arms in front of his chest.

"Look." She pulled a small electronic tablet out of her purse and made her way toward him as she tapped on the screen. She held up a picture of what looked to be some fancy hall decorated to look like an old barn. Or maybe it was an old barn cleaned up to look like a fancy hall. "People actually pay thousands of dollars to rent out aged buildings just like these for private events."

"Yeah, but how much work would it take to make this—" Cole gestured to the brick walls and windows caked with years of grime before pointing at her device "—look like *that*?"

"I guess it would depend on how motivated you were. I bet a cleaning crew could have this place scrubbed down in a couple of days. The roof might need some repairing, just in case it rains during the event, and you'll probably need a new shed door. I'm not an expert at refurbishing old buildings, but you'd only need to make it structurally sound, not livable. Part of the charm is in keeping the thing as rustic as possible. Then you bring in your own tables and chairs, or you get them from a party rental company, call up a caterer and go from there."

"Can I see that picture?" Lydia asked as she and Zach huddled together on one side of Vivienne. Cole found himself practically pressed up against her other side so that he could still see the screen as she swiped through similar images. But instead of focusing on the photos, his eyes kept straying toward the V-neck of her dress. Again.

Lydia's gasp caused his head to jerk up, an innocent expression pasted all over his guilty face. But instead of accusing him of ogling the wedding planner, his soon-to-be sister-in-law said excitedly, "You know what would be perfect? We should have our reception here. Just think! It would serve a dual purpose of celebrating our wedding and formally welcoming the Daltons to Rust Creek Falls."

"I love it," Vivienne gushed, before looking down at a text that popped up on her tablet. Unlike Zach and Lydia, who had stepped back and were too busy making googly eyes at each other and the derelict building, Cole was still right by Vivienne's side and could easily see the message.

You better be getting more bookings while you're there, or else. Her finger quickly swiped to hide the notification, but as soon as it was gone, a second one popped up. This time, there were no words. Just a row of dollar signs.

Luckily, he was able to look away right before she turned her head in his direction, probably hoping he hadn't seen her boss's directive. Even though his instincts had now been confirmed, there was something about the threat at the end that evoked just the smallest pang of sympathy.

Once, he'd had an old blowhard of a first sergeant who'd gotten in his face and cussed him up one side and down the other when he caught Cole helping another recruit clean the latrine. The dressing-down took place in front of the entire platoon, who all did their best to pretend nothing out of the ordinary was happening. So he was familiar with being embarrassed by high-handed bosses who never appreciated a job well-done. If only Estelle of Estelle's Events could see that her employee was currently reeling in her clients hook, line and sinker.

Still. Someone had to look out for his brother and make sure nobody was taking advantage of the lovestruck groom. Cole couldn't tamp down the need to remind the couple of the more practical side of things.

"I know you guys are thinking with your hearts right now, but maybe you should be thinking with your checking accounts." Honestly, Cole had no idea what their budget was, but every time Vivienne had made a suggestion during the car ride over here, he'd been reminded of one of those bar-code scanning machines in the grocery store, each beep signaling a rising total.

"Like I said, I'm not sure how much it would cost to get the building fixed up, but if you're not tearing it down, you'd likely be investing that much money into the place anyway to use it as a barn or a shed-thing or… whatever you would use it for on a ranch." Vivienne was definitely a city girl, all right. Yet she didn't let her lack of knowledge about cattle operations keep her from continuing on. "The table and chair rental will depend on what your final guest count is, but I have a vendor who includes linens and delivery and setup in the cost. Using a caterer is going to give you more flexibility with the menu than you might have at a restaurant or hotel. The flowers, the music, the cake and the photographer are all separate businesses you'd be hiring out anyway, so the location wouldn't matter. If you give me a day or so, I can draw up a new budget for you with some projected prices, but based on my experience, it'll be at least a few thousand dollars cheaper to have the reception here rather than using a formal venue."

Wait. Did Vivienne just say *cheaper*? As in she was trying to *save* Zach and Lydia money? And the woman was smiling as if she was actually happy to take a cut on her commission. Assuming she was working off a commission. Cole had no idea how people were paid in her line of work or why anyone would ever need to hire a wedding planner in the first place. It wasn't like it was a real job that required much effort.

His head spun at the whirlwind of conflicting thoughts and he tried to make sense of it all.

But when he saw his brother and Lydia walking around the space, eagerly talking about where they could put a dance floor and whether they should forgo a church ceremony and say their vows under the canopy of aspen trees outside, the weight of determination settled in Cole's chest. The Daltons, or at least their branch of the family, hadn't had anything to celebrate in a long time. So if having the party here gave Zach even a glimmer of happiness, then Cole was going to make sure the bride and groom had the biggest and best wedding the town of Rust Creek Falls had ever seen.

## Chapter Four

Estelle was going to have a fit about their company doing a "cowboy" wedding, Vivienne thought to herself as she drove toward Rust Creek Falls on a Sunday morning three weeks later. But ever since she'd seen that beautiful brick freight house, her brain had been buzzing with all kinds of ideas and she hadn't felt this motivated at work in a long time.

When Cole had made that comment about checking accounts and the cost of the Grant-Dalton wedding, Vivienne was certain that he'd seen Estelle's text to her about locking in more wedding contracts while she was in Rust Creek Falls. Then, out of nowhere, he'd all of a sudden switched gears and was promising that they could have the buildings on the family's new property ready within a month after closing.

The guy was a complete mystery to her. One minute, he was all stoic, chastising his brother for not having his cell phone on. The next minute, he was winking at her and calling her *ma'am* in that sexy drawl of his. Then he was suggesting that weddings were a waste of money right before volunteering to remodel the old washroom in the back of the freight house and turn it into a ladies' restroom.

Vivienne was used to unexpected changes and rolling with the flow. Both her childhood and her job had trained her well. But it'd sure be nice if Cole would pick a lane.

When she made a right onto the long driveway for Sawmill Station, she immediately noticed that there was a lush green lawn in place of the overgrown fields and there was freshly laid gravel preventing her compact car from landing in a pothole. But the biggest surprise of all was the crisp white paint on the clapboards of the train depot.

Vivienne's fingers froze on the gearshift as she put it in Park. No, the biggest surprise was seeing the sexy and unpredictable Cole Dalton on the roof of the depot, hammering in new shingles. He turned to look in her direction, and she took a few steadying breaths as he pulled a small, blue square of fabric from his back jeans pocket and wiped his forehead.

She thought about grabbing her phone or tablet and pretending she was busy on a call or returning emails, but Cole had obviously already caught her staring at him, because he was now descending the ladder propped up against the side of the building. Vivienne's mouth went dry. The tool belt slung low across his hips caused her gaze to focus on that area of his body and she reached up to make sure her sunglasses were still covering her eyes.

Reminding herself that she was a professional, Vivienne sucked in one last gulp of air and climbed out of her car. Instead of the straw cowboy hat she'd seen on him before, he was wearing a bright green ball cap, and judging by the dampness of his thin white tee, he'd ditched his usual flannel work shirt long ago. Just below the edge of his short sleeve, a tattoo peeked out with the letters *USMC*.

She swallowed as he walked toward her, wiping his hands on the back of his jeans. Vivienne told her muscles to unclench and tried for a casual greeting. "I can't believe how far along you guys are."

"Thanks. My brothers and I have been working around the clock to get the place in shape for the wedding. Personally, I don't see why Zach and Lydia are so hell-bent on rushing things along, but I figure the sooner we get them off on their honeymoon, the sooner the rest of us can get to work on actually building the main house and setting up for the cattle."

"Well, three more weeks and I'll be out of your hair for good." Vivienne's smile hardly slipped out of place. She'd planned weddings in shorter amounts of time, so it wasn't like this was much of a challenge for her. But she'd also never had Estelle breathing down her neck about bringing in more business while simultaneously having to fight her attraction to one of her client's brothers.

Confusion marred his brow for a brief moment before he jerked his chin toward her empty arms and asked, "Where's your trusty binder?"

"Oh. It's in the back. I'm supposed to meet Lydia here at noon, but I wanted to come early and set up a few decoration samples for her to decide on so I can place orders. Do you know if the electrical stuff is finished inside the freight house? I brought some strings of lights I wanted to test out."

"That was one of the first things we got sorted out." He tapped on the cordless drill holstered inside his tool belt. "You know men and their power tools."

Actually, what Vivienne knew about handyman cowboys wouldn't even fill a shot glass. And with how dry her mouth had grown in the last sixty seconds, she could sure use a shot of something right now.

They were facing each other over the hood of her Jetta and, since Cole didn't seem to be in any hurry to return to work, she stammered, "So, uh, I'll just head on over to the freight house and let you get back to your roof."

He tipped his cap but didn't turn away.

"Okay, then." Vivienne gave an awkward nod and pivoted toward the rear of her car, using her remote to pop open the trunk. She'd just go about her business and, hopefully, Cole would get the hint that he should go about his.

Instead, the sound of crunching gravel followed her, and she felt the heat of his nearby presence as she stared at the cardboard box of mason jars and stacks of table runners. "Here, let me help you carry this stuff."

Before she could refuse his offer, he'd already stepped in front of her and hefted out a roll of burlap and a spool of twinkling lights. "You don't have to do that. I can get it..."

Her protest died as he walked off, balancing his loads under each rounded bicep. As she watched his backside, her heart skipped several beats before she grabbed a centerpiece in each hand and rushed to catch up. Thank goodness she'd learned her lesson about wearing heels out here in the country. Today she'd thrown on her favorite pair of Chuck Taylors after choosing an outfit that she didn't mind getting dirty.

Fortunately, the freight house was no longer dirty at all. In fact, the windows had been thoroughly scrubbed—with several broken ones replaced—and the floors had been swept out. The cobwebs were long gone and the place was no longer littered with rodent droppings. "Wow. This is even better than I'd expected."

Cole set his load down in a corner before taking the flowers out of her hands. "Are you serious? It looks like an empty old warehouse in here."

"I know! That's the look we're going for."

Doubt flashed in his cool blue eyes, but his only response was a slight shake of his head. "I guess you're the wedding expert."

"Trust me." This time *she* gave *him* the saucy wink, then spun around and hurried back to the car before he could see the heat staining her cheeks.

They didn't speak again until they'd brought everything inside, which took only two more trips, since the man could carry more than half his body weight in tea-light candles. Vivienne did a mental inventory to make sure she hadn't forgotten anything, then stopped short.

"Hey, Cole, Zach picked up a banquet and sixty-inch round from the office a few days ago. Do you know where he put them?"

He took off his cap and ran his hand through his short black hair. "I have no idea what you just said."

"They're tables." Vivienne extended her arms as far as they'd go. "One's sixty inches in diameter. The other is a long rectangle for banquet seating."

"Right. I don't speak wedding." He just spoke power tools. And probably trucks and cattle and semper fi. "We stored them inside the depot when we sealed the concrete floor in here. I'll grab them for you."

"I can help." She might not have broad shoulders or sinewy forearms or six-pack abs like him, however, she'd certainly carried her fair share of folding tables. Okay, so maybe she wasn't exactly sure about his abs, but his shirt was thin and tight enough to suggest that there might be a few ridges underneath.

Vivienne quickly caught up alongside him so that she wouldn't be forced to examine his body as they made their way to the depot. He opened the blue door, which had been painted to match the large sliding shed-style doors on the freight house, and extended his arm, indicating she should enter first. A shiver shot down her spine as she wondered if he was now going to be the one studying her from behind.

The depot was a one-room building, only about nine hundred square feet, with a long, dusty counter dividing the majority of the space from the back wall. She pointed to a small enamel basin affixed to a corner with some broken pieces of wood framing out a square around it. "Does that sink work?"

"It might have at one point, since we found some pipes running from that corner to the main water line. Our best guess is that someone had started building an indoor restroom for the public to use, but then business tanked and the thing never got finished."

Vivienne tapped her chin with two fingers, looking between the fixture and the counter. "How hard would it be to install a bigger sink? Only temporarily?"

"Why would someone only need a temporary sink?"

"I was thinking that the caterers could work out of here."

"You want us to build you a kitchen?"

"Not for me. For the caterers. And not an actual kitchen. That would be terribly expensive and would probably require building permits. With only three weeks to go, nobody has time for that. But with the counter already here and a bigger sink, the caterers could do some of the food prep and staging here, which would save time and cut down on costs."

"I suppose we could do that."

She swiveled in his direction, her palms held up. "Unless you guys had another plan on how to use this building."

"Well, since we can't bulldoze it because it's a landmark and it's too small for a stable, I have absolutely no idea how to put it to good use on a ranch. I'll ask around and find you a bigger sink."

For the first time all morning, Vivienne's smile wasn't forced when she looked at him. "Thank you."

"I'm glad to help." His eyes lowered to her lips and a rush of warmth swirled in her tummy. She told herself to take a step back, but her feet stayed planted where they were. Instead, her gaze dropped to his mouth and when the corner tilted up into a knowing smirk, Vivienne gasped.

The short intake of air startled her back to reality and she recovered by clearing her throat. "I should probably head outside to get away from all this dust."

Whipping around to the door, she took several purposeful strides, praying that he wouldn't notice how shaky her legs had suddenly become. Cole's voice stopped her when she got to the threshold. "Aren't you forgetting something?"

"Like what?" she asked, making a pretense of searching her surroundings for forgotten items, without actually turning around and facing him again. She'd definitely left her pride behind somewhere, but she bit back that response.

"The banquet and sixty-inch round?"

She narrowed her eyes before realization dawned. The tables. The whole reason for coming in here with him in the first place. "Of course."

Luckily she needed to take only a couple steps back before she could cut a diagonal path to the front wall where they were propped. She started to roll the bigger one, then froze when his hand covered hers. "I didn't mean for you to take them with you. I planned to carry them. I just needed you to tell me where they go."

"I can help," she said, rotating inward to slip her hand out from under his warm, strong fingers. But the maneuver was a mistake, because she hadn't anticipated how close he was behind her and she ended up two inches away from the wall of his chest. And he still hadn't released her hand, preventing her from moving too far. She inhaled deeply, catching his scent of fabric softener and hardworking male.

"Let me do it for you," he replied, his voice low and his breath a soft caress against her forehead.

Tilting her face back, she melted under the intensity of his eyes and couldn't look away. Vivienne no longer knew what he wanted to do for her, but she parted her mouth, about to allow him full access.

Cole moved in closer, his head dipping down toward hers. But before his lips could make contact, a horn blasted outside.

Cole couldn't believe he'd been right about to kiss the wedding planner before the boisterous caravan of his extended family honked their arrival. He'd known his aunt Rita and uncle Charles had told all of his cousins that everyone was going to pitch in today to help get things finished in time. Just like an old-fashioned barn raising. Minus the barn.

But he hadn't expected them all so soon. Of course, he also hadn't expected to get distracted by pretty Vivienne Shuster.

They'd both jumped apart so quickly when that first horn sounded, the table they'd been fighting for control over almost went crashing down to the floor. Then her face had turned a charming shade of crimson, and she'd blinked several times before whirling toward the door and leaving him holding the sixty-inch round.

Now, two hours later, Cole watched her from his perch on top of the rafters in the freight house, where he'd been hanging all these ridiculous twinkly lights. Uncle Charles had volunteered to string the things up, but Cole couldn't very well let his father's older brother risk breaking his neck by climbing up and down the ladder so many times.

Plus, it gave Cole an excuse to stay inside where Vivienne was busy working. She was fifteen feet below him, standing with Lydia and Aunt Rita as they surveyed the different table settings she'd arranged. From up here, all the plates and flowers and different-colored tablecloths looked like a bunch of fuss. But judging by the way the other women were oohing and aahing over Vivienne's displays, it was evident that she must be fairly good at her job. Not that he was any clearer on what exactly her job was.

But she certainly knew how to orchestrate all his relatives to do her bidding. And she was so subtle and diplomatic about it, doing that chin-tapping thing, tilting her pretty little head and wondering out loud about a possibility; half of them hadn't even noticed that she was adding to their workload. In fact, right this second, his baby brother Shawn and his cousins Eli and Derek were at the lumberyard in town buying up a truck bed full of wood because Vivienne had suggested that a gazebo would be perfect between the two aspen trees outside.

Booker, his oldest brother, and Zach were proving

their lack of plumbing skills by installing a new sink and vanity in the old freight office, which was currently undergoing renovations to be turned into a restroom for guests.

Wherever there was a broken-down mess, or even just a plain, empty space, Vivienne Shuster had an idea of how to improve upon it—usually in the most simple and inexpensive way. More important, she had an uncanny knack of relaying her vision with so much enthusiasm that everyone was eager to see it to fruition.

Hell, even he'd offered to build her a kitchen inside a hundred-year-old shack that had been nothing but an eyesore only a month ago. Still. Annoyance had prickled at his skin every time one of his single male relatives jumped at the opportunity to impress her. Not that he was jealous or anything. It wasn't like he *wanted* to be attracted to her. He certainly had no intention of acting on that attraction, despite how close he'd come to doing just that inside the train depot. It was simply that he didn't want anyone else helping her carry tables.

Hooking the staple gun onto his belt, Cole surveyed the final strand of lights and called out, "Okay, Dad, plug them in."

But the bulbs stayed unlit.

"Dad?" Cole braced his hands on the wooden beam so he could lean over and search for the older man.

"Phil's outside with Garrett," Uncle Charles offered as he navigated a huge box strapped to a dolly. "They're looking at the old train tracks, trying to figure out how to make them safe so that nobody trips over them."

Lord, all his family needed was to have one of the

partygoers indulge in too much of Homer Gilmore's spiked punch—which had been rumored to be responsible for many Rust Creek Falls weddings not too long ago—and risk twisting their ankles or doing a face-plant on the Dalton property.

As he climbed down the ladder rungs, Cole made a mental note to look into whether they might need an extra insurance policy. He shook his head. "And Dad thinks *Garrett* is the best one to come up with a safe solution?"

Uncle Charles shrugged and replied, "He's pretty mechanical. Besides, everyone else was already working on something."

"This is an accident waiting to happen," Cole muttered to himself, and since he was striding past the women as he said it, three sets of eyes turned to look at him.

Vivienne handed a mason jar full of flowers over to Lydia and said, "You guys talk over which option you like best. We can always use the burlap for the chair sashes if you'd rather have the linen runners on the tables."

Cole continued past them, but before he knew it, Vivienne was matching his pace and gave his arm a gentle tug. Her soft touch caused him to almost lose all sense of direction and he slowed down.

"What's wrong?" she asked, her voice hushed as her concerned eyes darted back toward Lydia. While Cole appreciated the fact that Vivienne didn't want to worry his soon-to-be sister-in-law, this new development was a pretty big deal.

"Oh, nothing. Except for the fact that we have half a mile of broken-down railroad tracks all over our property, and someone thought it would be a good idea to get a bunch of people wearing high heels and slick cowboy boots together at night, serve gallons of rum punch and then send them out to walk around in the dark."

"But Garrett said he could fix it."

"Clearly you don't know my brother."

When they got to the door, he looked at Vivienne in time to see her eyes widen and her throat constrict as she swallowed. "Enlighten me."

"Garrett would just as soon build a roller coaster on those tracks rather than pull them up. Wait." He stopped when they got outside and planted himself in front of her. "Can we even pull the things up? Are they part of the landmark preservation thing my dad agreed to?"

Her only response was to bite her lower lip, again reminding him of the fact that he'd almost kissed her earlier today. What had he been thinking? What had any of them been thinking?

He groaned and continued walking. "Man, I can't believe we didn't do something about this sooner."

"Cole," she said, catching up to him again. "There's always a workable solution."

He kept walking. "Did they teach you that in wedding-planner college?"

"No. Life taught me that. And just for the record, my degree is in business administration. Wedding planning is only my fallback career."

Cole drew up short, immediately feeling like a jerk for making the snide remark. Especially because he knew what it was like to have a fallback career. If it were up to him, he'd still be in the Marine Corps. He'd also still have his mom here, but he couldn't go back in time and fix the past. He could only solve today's problems.

Guilt washed through him. "Sorry. That was a crappy thing to say. I didn't mean to insult your profession."

"Listen, you're not the first family member I've dealt with who thought hiring an event company was a waste of money." Her smile would've been more reassuring if it matched her eyes.

"I know I acted that way at first, but you've really taken a lot of the pressure off my brother and Lydia. I know they're both overwhelmed with throwing this thing, and you're so good with Lydia, giving her ideas and suggestions without bullying her into what *you* think she should have."

"Thank you," she said, this time looking as though she meant it. "Now, let me do my job."

Vivienne walked toward the platform of the depot, where Garrett was lying down on his belly next to the side of the track and using one open eye and an extended hand to measure something off in the distance. His dad was resting his hands on top of a shovel handle, his forehead planted on his stacked fingers as he shook his head at whatever Garrett was saying.

"Hey there, gentlemen," she said sweetly as they drew near. "Have you guys come up with any clever solutions so far?"

Garrett jumped to his feet and dusted the dirt and gravel off his belly. "Well, I was thinking we could find a couple of those old mining carts and use them to ferry the guests back and forth from the parking area to the freight house."

A vein throbbed in Cole's temple and he squeezed his lids shut.

"Hmm." Vivienne nodded, as if she was seriously contemplating his brother's asinine suggestion. "You mean like one of those handcar things with the crank that people pump up and down to make it move?"

"Actually, I meant one of those huge carts with the sides about so high." Garrett gestured toward his chest. "The ones that miners used to fill up with coal and supplies and stuff. Then we could harness it to one of the horses and pull people inside, kind of like an old-fashioned buggy ride—except on the rails so they can haul butt. To be honest, though, your idea of the hand-cart sounds way more fun."

"I think they both sound fun," Vivienne stated, and Cole rolled his eyes, ready to interject. "However, you could probably only operate one or two at a time, and at last count the guest list was pushing two hundred. That's a lot of shuttle trips back and forth and people won't want to wait. Would it be difficult to turn the tracks into some sort of walkway? Maybe use cement or dirt or something to pack between the two rails so that the metal part is still showing, keeping the old-fashioned charm, but making it more of an outline of a modern sidewalk?"

His father's face slowly lifted and Garrett's eyes lit up. In fact, Cole's own head tilted as he considered that possibility.

Vivienne continued. "But all of you have already done so much work in such a short amount of time and I don't want you to do anything to your property that you're not comfortable with."

"I know I don't want to tiptoe around these tracks and risk falling down and breaking my old neck," Phil Dalton said. "Sounds like a good enough plan to me."

"But if we turn it into a sidewalk, we won't be able to use any handcarts on the tracks. Don't you think it'd be kinda cool to have races and stuff with them?" Garrett was enthusiastically bobbing his head up and down and Cole opened his mouth to tell his brother that he shouldn't leave the house without a helmet.

Fortunately, Vivienne spoke before him. "There's still the track on the back side of the freight house. You can set up your handcarts over there. After the reception is over, obviously."

"Obviously," their dad repeated, his eyes drilled in Garrett's direction, as if to drive home the implication that there weren't going to be any carts or any racing at any time during the wedding.

Cole had to admit it—the woman really was brilliant at solving problems without making others feel as though she was steering them in a direction they didn't want to go. And before he knew it, she was steering him back toward the freight house. "Let's go plug in those lights."

Cole tossed a smug smile in his brother's direction before eagerly following along.

## Chapter Five

"Where did those come from?" Vivienne asked the oldest Dalton brother as he rolled two old-fashioned barrels on either side of him through the freight house. What was his name again? Booker? She needed a chart to keep track of all the relatives.

"They were stacked in a storage room built behind the office. After we moved them, we found a trapdoor hidden in the floor and Lydia thinks that the former owners might've operated a still down there during Prohibition. The Dumpster is already full, so I'm going to load them in my truck and find somewhere to get rid of them."

"No, they're perfect. Can I have them?"

"For what?" Cole asked her. He'd already had her all flustered after that near kiss in the depot. While she worked, she didn't need him following her around second-guessing everything she was doing.

She was saved from responding by the sound of another car horn outside. Was that a Rust Creek Falls thing? Why did everyone who drove up have to honk their arrival?

"Food's here!" Charles slapped his palms together as he came out of the freight office area. "After we eat, you guys should go check out the moonshine room."

An idea flickered, but Rita Dalton was waving everyone outside, barking orders to her sons and nephews to help set up the tables. Vivienne would have to give this so-called moonshine room a little more thought.

"Uncle Ben and Aunt Mary are right behind us," the newly arrived driver said. Two more women she thought might be Rita's daughters carried boxes advertising Buffalo Bart's Wings-To-Go, and Vivienne found herself standing in the center of the gravel lot as Dalton after Dalton sped by her, unloading wooden benches and two picnic tables and dozens of assorted containers of what looked to be homemade side dishes.

It felt odd not to be the one giving direction as the whirlwind of activity happened around her. She was used to crowds at other weddings or parties, but this was different. It was all one family. And they were huge. And overwhelming. And loud. But in a good way.

She startled when Cole's hand touched her lower back. He leaned to whisper, "You better get in line before all the chicken is gone."

Vivienne's stomach rumbled. She had a healthy appetite and could put away a fair amount of food. But looking at the heaping platters and salad-filled bowls, she calculated that it would take even this brood at least three days to consume all of it.

"C'mon, Vivienne," Rita called, holding out a paper plate.

Feeling everyone's eyes on her, Vivienne carefully scooped out small amounts of potato salad, coleslaw, green beans and sliced watermelon. The chicken looked incredible, but she limited herself to three boneless strips. Then she saw the pan of corn bread and her tummy told her that she would feel so much more at ease if she topped off her plate with a hunk the size of her fist. By the time she got to the end of the table, all the other women had filed in behind her, following her lead.

She took her food toward one of the benches set up under the shade of the aspen trees, balancing her full plate on her knees, since many of the guys were lounging around the other picnic table waiting for their turn in line. Rita and Lydia came next, and the rest of the ladies joined them on nearby benches. Cole and Booker were the last ones to get their food and most of the seats were taken by that point, with some of the men standing up to eat.

There was about a foot of space left next to her, and Booker made his way toward it, as though he intended to squeeze in beside her. But right before he could sit down, Cole appeared with his elbows outstretched and rammed his body between Vivienne and Booker, causing his brother to drop his plate as Cole slammed himself onto the bench hard enough to jostle the opposite end.

"Darn it, Cole," Rita said, recovering from the

bounce and wiping her mouth on a paper napkin. "This isn't a teeter-totter."

Cole was pressed up so close against Vivienne's arm that her own paper plate was in danger of folding in on itself. But instead of an apology, he looked smugly at his big brother while the rest of the Dalton men hooted and laughed.

"Gotta be quicker than that, Booker," Garrett catcalled.

"Hey, Lydia," Zach, who was standing with the other men, hollered to his fiancé. "Why don't we play musical chairs at the reception? If we put our money on Cole, we could probably win enough bets to pay for the whole wedding."

"Nah," Shawn Dalton said. "Cole'll only compete if there's a pretty wedding planner in the open seat."

Heat flooded Vivienne's face and Cole threw a buttermilk biscuit at Shawn, who was too busy doubling over with laughter to duck.

"You boys mind your manners," Rita said in a firm, authoritative voice. Then she turned to Vivienne as the guffaws were smothered into mere snickers and smirks. "Honey, don't pay them any mind."

Cole's shoulder remained pressed against hers, and each time he took a bite, she felt his movement. There was no way he could be comfortable sitting so close to her on such a small area of wood. But the man didn't budge. It was almost as if he needed to prove to his relatives that he wasn't the least bit affected by their teasing. Or maybe he truly wasn't bothered by it. Which meant Vivienne shouldn't be bothered by the comments, either, especially the one about him wanting the seat by the wedding planner.

Surely, the only reason he was sitting here was because it was the last spot left, and he'd been working long before everyone else got there, so he was probably exhausted. Or perhaps he was only sitting here because he had an inherent need to compete and beat one of his brothers out of something. That had to be it. With his straight spine and cocky expression, Cole resembled a bridesmaid who'd just beat out every other single woman trying to catch the bride's bouquet.

Which reminded Vivienne to get back to business. "Lydia, did your maid of honor pick up her dress yet?"

"Yes, and Joanna says hers fits perfectly," Lydia said, referring to her childhood friend. "Jolene tried hers on at the *Gazette* office and has been talking about matching accessories at work nonstop. And Eva dropped hers off with the tailor yesterday."

Vivienne clenched her jaw at the mention of Eva-Rose Armstrong's name but tried not to show her concern. Most brides didn't ask one of their groom's prior dates to be part of the wedding party, and Vivienne could only hope that Lydia was right and that the woman Zach once went out with had happily moved on with the new man in her life.

"How are you going to wear your hair, dear?" Aunt Mary asked Lydia, who gave a helpless shrug.

"I don't know. What do you think, Vivienne?"

Out of all the women here, most of them their own age, Lydia had asked her. Pride blossomed in Vivienne's chest, knowing it was the ultimate vote of confidence when a bride valued her opinion. Sitting up straighter, she accidentally rammed her elbow into Cole's steely bicep. He didn't even flinch.

"It depends on how formal you want to look," Vivienne said, knowing that Lydia rarely wore makeup and preferred to keep her brown curls loose and casual.

"I want it to look natural, but I also want it to be special."

"Well, I have mobile beauticians and makeup artists on speed dial if you want to go that route. Or we can keep business local and use Bee's Beauty Parlor in town. In either event, we should probably pull up some styles that you'd prefer and ask around." Vivienne tapped her chin before continuing on. "Actually, I was kind of toying with the idea of a little theme and I think it would work well with your dress."

Lydia's face brightened. "I love a theme. What is it?"

"Well, you guys found what might've been an old still and with the hundred-year-old train depot and your work at the newspaper, we could do sort of a Prohibition era 1920s revival thing. I'm not thinking of a full-on speakeasy and flappers doing the Charleston. But maybe some subtle touches to complement the property's history."

"It's like you know exactly what I want before I could possibly even think of it," Lydia gushed, making Vivienne's chest fill with satisfaction.

But the satisfaction was short-lived as everyone else began chiming in with their own ideas. Some of them were good; however, some of them had Lydia crinkling her nose.

One of the female Dalton cousins clapped her hands.

"Ooh, we could dress the ring bearers up like little newsies with tweed derby hats. They could pass out programs and yell, 'Extra, extra, read all about it.' How adorable would that be?"

"What about the groomsmen?" Garrett asked, his eyes bright and energized. "Can we get zoot suits and tommy guns?"

Vivienne tried to tamp down the panic wedging in her throat. She should've waited to talk to Lydia and Zach alone about a decision this size. Once again, it was time to rein things in.

Leaning forward to look around Cole, who was still squished up beside her and shoveling food into his mouth, Vivienne asked Zach, "Didn't you already decide what color tuxes you wanted? If you're using that rental company I suggested, we're going to need to get everyone fitted as soon as possible."

"Whoa." Shawn held up his plastic fork like a stop sign. "I'm not wearing a tux."

Cole's upper arm brushed against hers as he swiveled in his seat and planted both boots on either side of the edge of the bench to face his brother. "Who says you even get to be in the wedding?"

"I say," Shawn replied. "As long as I don't have to put on a monkey suit or slow dance with any of the bridesmaids."

"Yeah, entertaining the ladies isn't exactly in your wheelhouse, Shawn. I believe that's *my* specialty." Garrett might've been the one speaking, but the wall of Cole's back pressed up against her side prevented Vivienne from seeing much of the playful banter going on in that direction. "In fact, that's why Zach wants *me* to be the best man."

"I do?" Zach asked.

Vivienne's pulse sped up and she turned questioning eyes toward Lydia. *Please say you've already decided this.* But the woman looked as clueless as Vivienne felt.

"I doubt it, Garrett," Cole argued. "You're the most likely to lose the ring."

Shawn laughed. "That's right. Dad, remember when Garrett forgot me at the county fair that one year? You put him in charge of buying me a corn dog, but then he ditched me to go on the Scream Xtreme with Rondalee... What's her name? You know, the girl who had the big—" Shawn cupped his hands to his chest and Phil interrupted him with a severe shake of his head. "I was going to say tomatoes, Dad. She won the blue ribbon in gardening that year."

"I didn't *lose* you," Garrett defended. "You wandered off and Cole found you in one of the 4-H pens trying to feed cotton candy to the goats."

"That's right." Cole stood up abruptly and Vivienne almost toppled over. "*I* was the one who found you. And then *I* called the vet for those poor goats. Lydia, trust me, you don't want these two ensuring things go right on your big day."

"If you ask me, it's simple." Booker looked up from the table where he was getting a third helping of food— well, only a second helping if one didn't count the plate Cole had made him drop. "I'm the oldest, so I get to be the best man."

Vivienne saw the muscles in Cole's chest expand as

he drew in a gulp of air. He exhaled on a sigh. "Zach, do you recall Booker's valedictorian speech in high school? We spent years trying to get the teachers to forget we were related to him. Would you really want him giving the best man toast?"

Zach's only response was to laugh. Phil Dalton hitched up his belt and said, "Well, sons, there's only one way to settle this."

Someone whooped and one of the cousins produced a bucket of metal horseshoes. Vivienne leaned toward Rita to ask, "What are they doing?"

"They're going to play a game of horseshoes to decide." The older woman shook her head. "Just be glad they haven't moved any of the steers or horses out here yet. The last thing this wedding needs is someone showing up with a broken leg after a bronc-riding contest."

When someone hammered a metal stake into the ground, Lydia stood up and Vivienne asked, "Is this really happening?"

Lydia smiled. "Welcome to Rust Creek Falls."

"Let me go grab my tape measure," Cole said when Zach tried to count out the distance between the two stakes. Garrett had upended one of the wooden benches to use as a backstop, before his aunt Mary told him to put it back and find a scrap of wood somewhere else.

When Cole returned, he had his tool belt slung over one shoulder and Vivienne's tote bag in his hand. "Your purse was ringing in the freight house, so I thought you might need it."

She looked at the missed-call log and saw Estelle's name listed several times. And, apparently, so had Cole, who was still standing right next to her. She offered him a weak smile and said, "It's no big deal. I can call her back."

Cole gave her a terse nod before joining his brothers. She was glad one of the Dalton cousins outlined the rules, because Vivienne had no idea how the game was played. Lydia reminded everyone that they still had a building they needed to get ready for a wedding, so it was decided they'd do only one round with two pitches each. The brother with the best score would win.

Setting her tote bag on the abandoned bench, Vivienne joined the rest of the spectators at the makeshift horseshoe pit. She watched intently as each Dalton took his turn, with Phil and Charles measuring who came closest.

She found herself holding her breath when Cole opted to pitch last. His first horseshoe easily spun around the stake and his second landed less than an inch away. Excitement bubbled through her when Zach announced that Cole was the winner and she was surprised to realize that she'd been secretly rooting for him all along.

Instead of pumping his fist in the air or making macho whooping sounds like other guys might do when they won, the newly designated best man simply spun on his boot and looked directly at her. She finally recognized the look that had been on his face earlier when he'd beaten his older brother to the spot on the bench.

It was triumph.

"We want a rematch!" Booker and Garrett shouted at the same time.

Shawn took a more subtle approach by directing his

appeal toward Lydia. "I hope you know you're making a big mistake by reinforcing Sergeant Save-the-Day's ego."

In all of the weddings she'd planned, none of them had needed an athletic competition to decide who was going to head up the wedding party. Maybe Estelle had been right to warn her about doing cowboy weddings.

And speaking of Estelle, Vivienne's phone chimed with the distinctive ring tone she'd chosen for her boss—the whistle from the Hunger Games movie series—and she reached into her bag to switch the thing to vibrate. But not before Cole looked at her and saw what she was doing. She was tempted to turn it off completely, but she remembered the Daltons' rule about phone accessibility and didn't want to inadvertently offend anyone again.

Vivienne slid the cell into the side compartment of her bag just as Cole walked toward her. "Is everything okay?"

"Yep. We should probably start cleaning up over here and get back to work," Vivienne told him, but it was difficult to keep a neutral expression when her bag began vibrating.

Cole tilted his head. "Maybe you should take that."

She bit back a retort that maybe he should mind his own business. After all, even she had to concede that it would appear beyond unprofessional to blatantly ignore her boss. "Excuse me," she murmured to him before turning her back and sliding her finger across the screen to accept the call.

"Hello?"

"Have you scored us any more bookings out there in the backwoods?" Estelle's gravelly voice was louder than ever, and Vivienne frantically searched for the button to turn down the volume on her earpiece before anyone could overhear.

"Oh, hey there, Estelle. I'm, um, on-site for the Grant-Dalton wedding. Can I give you a call back later this afternoon?" Vivienne hoped the subtle statement would be enough to remind her boss that she wasn't in a position to be talking about drumming up more business.

But Estelle launched into her without regard for who was nearby. "You promised me you'd deliver another client by now, but instead you're avoiding my calls and building barns on my dime. This is what happens when you don't use one of our prearranged venues and decide to get creative."

"It's an old train station, not a barn," Vivienne said through a semi-clenched jaw. The depot was the closest building, so she headed in that direction for some quick privacy.

"Is it a new client, though, or is it the same cattle rustlers you brought to the office last month?"

"Estelle, you know that I'm doing my best—"

"I know nothing of the sort. You're over there in the latest marriage capital of Montana and you still can't bring me another viable customer? I took a chance on you when you were a fresh-faced kid out of business school and I expected great things from you. I poured a lot of energy into training you, going out of my way to introduce you to vendors, putting my own reputation on the line every time you came up with some harebrained plan to do things different and trendy. At minimum, I would like a return on my investment."

Vivienne reached the front door of the depot right as the tears threatened to fill her eyes. "I assure you that I am working on several leads and—"

"Leads aren't good enough," Estelle snapped. "I need results."

"And I'll have results. Just give me another week."

"You have twenty-four hours to get another booking or you're fired."

Cole was probably the biggest jerk of all for following Vivienne inside when she so clearly was trying to avoid having anyone overhear her phone call. But she'd looked so concerned and nervous, which was completely opposite to the controlled and capable image she usually projected. As the newly appointed best man, his primary job was to ensure that this wedding went off without a hitch. And if that meant seeing to the wedding planner, then so be it.

"You okay?" Cole asked her when she bit her cheeks, her eyes looking up, as though she was trying to decide how much to tell him.

"I'm fine. I was just startled to see you in here, that's all."

"Is that really all?" He cocked his head.

She leaned against the old countertop and gave a nervous chuckle that caught in her throat. "So you heard all that, huh?"

He nodded and she blew out a breath, causing one of the blond wavy locks that had escaped her ponytail to dance along her temple. "It sounded like you were in trouble with your boss."

"Trouble is an understatement. But it's nothing for anyone else to worry about."

"Could this affect Zach and Lydia's wedding?"

Vivienne's shoulders sagged and a look of defeat crossed her face. "I wish I could say it won't, but I'm pretty sure I'm about to be fired. Which doesn't necessarily mean that Lydia and Zach will be left in the lurch only three weeks before their wedding. Of course, they'll still have their contract with the company and my boss will honor it. But then they will have to work directly with Estelle and I doubt that will be a smooth transition."

Cole searched her face for some sort of indication that would tell him whether or not the woman was fishy or dishonest or unethical. He doubted it, but if she was, it was better she hop in her little Jetta now and drive away. "You said *about* to be fired? Did you do something illegal or break some wedding etiquette rule or something?"

"No!" Her hand flew to her chest, and a blush stole up her cheeks. "Nothing like that. It's just that my boss wants me to book another client."

"Is that all?" Cole's tension eased. "Then let's go out and talk to my cousins. Every time I turn around, somebody in this town is getting married. I'm sure they'll know someone else who might need a wedding planner."

Vivienne sighed. "I wish it were that easy."

"Seems simple enough to me."

"Weddings are very personal and special things,

and a couple should be comfortable with whoever they choose to be involved. Estelle wants a contract signed tomorrow and, in good conscience, I couldn't have someone rush into making that kind of commitment just to save my own job."

Cole studied her, one half of his brain telling him to keep his mouth shut before he said something stupid, the other half telling him that he was the only person who could fix this.

"So just to clarify… You only need to book *one* client?"

"For now, at least."

"For *one* wedding that can happen whenever?"

Her eyes narrowed with suspicion. "Correct."

"Then plan mine."

## Chapter Six

Vivienne felt the flurry of emotions cross her face, the most prominent one being disgust because all she could think of was how he'd almost kissed her before the rest of his family had shown up. Vivienne had to flatten her palm against the worn countertop to keep from curling it into a fist. "You're engaged?"

"Of course I'm not engaged." Cole visibly shuddered. "I'm not even boyfriend material, let alone husband material."

Confusion quickly replaced her anger and Vivienne could only stutter, "Wh-why?"

"I guess because I have more important things going on in my life right now than to cozy up to some female I'm not interested in and pretend like I give a damn about all this commitment crap."

"No, I mean why would you need to plan a wedding if you're not getting married?"

"You said you need to book another client." He rocked onto the heels of his boots. "Well, I'm your next client."

Vivienne shook her head as if she could jiggle all the scattered pieces of this puzzle into place. "A client who has no intention of getting married?"

"Yes. But it's not like your boss would know the difference."

"She might figure it out when no actual marriage takes place. If you're not boyfriend material, then does that mean you don't have a girlfriend? I mean, who would we say you're marrying?"

Okay, so that first question Vivienne threw in for her own clarification. Even though they hadn't exactly kissed, she needed reassurance that she wasn't lusting over some guy who was off-limits.

"Nope, no need for a girlfriend," he said, and she felt some of her apprehension drain. But then he took a couple of steps closer. "We can make something up, but why would it even need to get that far? Look, you just need to buy yourself some time to bring in more business. So you sign me up or whatever you need to do to get your boss off your back, and then after you bring in some more customers—legitimate ones—my fake fiancée will have cold feet and we'll call it off."

If her eyes squinted any more, they'd be squeezed shut. And then she'd miss his normal teasing smirk telling her that he was only kidding. But his jaw was locked into place and the set of his straight mouth looked dead serious.

"It would never work." She waved her hand at him, deciding one of them should try to write this whole conversation off as a joke.

"Why can't it?"

"Estelle requires a contract. Like the kind that's legally binding in a court of law."

"So I come into your office and sign the contract. There's got to be a cancellation clause in there somewhere. You can't tell me you guys have never had someone cancel their wedding before."

"There is. Which is why she demands a security deposit up front."

"What are we talking about? A hundred bucks? Two hundred? How do you get paid, anyway?"

"Fifteen hundred," Vivienne replied, then almost smiled as Cole's eyes went round.

"And only the bride and groom pay that?" he asked. "You don't get any kickbacks from the florist or the minister or everyone?"

"First of all, clergy members are only offered a small honorarium that they oftentimes donate to their house of worship. Second of all, do you think I'd take money from a minister?" She quickly put her hand up. "No. Don't answer that. It's not like I work off commission. We get paid for the amount of hours we spend working on your wedding. So if it's going to be a big event, plan to pay for at least eighty hours of my time. Even if you and your pretend fiancée require the smaller, twenty-hour package, it's still a hefty chunk of change."

"Right." The man shrugged as if the pickup truck he drove wasn't at least twenty years old. "I have some money saved up from when I was in the Marines. My dad didn't want me dipping into my personal savings to invest in the ranch, since it's supposed to be a family operation. It's not like I have anything else I need to spend it on."

They stood there staring at each other across the counter. Vivienne racked her brain for another flaw to his ridiculous suggestion. But she felt completely empty—drained of all emotion and rational thought. And with his determined stance and squared shoulders, Cole didn't seem to be the kind of man who backed down from anything.

"Why would you do something for someone you barely know?"

"I could give you a hundred reasons, from the fact that you haven't once tried to sell my brother something he doesn't need, to the fact that you're hardworking and not afraid to jump in and get your hands dirty. But the bottom line is that this wedding is important to Zach and Lydia. I need it to go smoothly and I'm convinced that you're the best person for the job."

Then why did Vivienne feel as if she was a complete fraud?

What Cole didn't tell Vivienne was that it almost tore his heart out to see her hiding inside the train depot, fighting back those tears. So maybe he'd been a little impulsive when he'd made his offer yesterday. But once he'd put it out there, he knew there was no turning back. No backing down.

Still, when he pulled up to her office the following morning, it took him a solid five minutes to convince himself that he could put on a courageous face and brave the feminine confines of Vivienne's office again. It might've been a slight exaggeration when Cole had told his brother that the place reminded him of a war zone; however, he definitely felt like he was going into a battle he didn't know how to fight.

Before he got out of his truck, he looked at his reflection in the rearview mirror. He'd done the right thing, hadn't he? A voice told him that if he was so convinced about what he was about to do, he would've mentioned something to his dad yesterday. Or even to Zach or Lydia. Yet he'd remained silent the remainder of the day, keeping to himself as the rest of his family followed Vivienne's advice on everything from landscaping to repurposing old wood. Cole had been sure to avoid her, because he knew that if he allowed her to dwell on his plan, she'd try to talk him out of it.

But what was he supposed to do? Let the woman get fired from her job? He grabbed his checkbook as he finally exited his truck. He wasn't protecting her, he reminded himself for the hundredth time. He was doing this to help his brother and Lydia.

Cole must've lingered in the parking lot too long, because before he could get to the entrance, Vivienne came sailing out the front door. "I was going to call you this morning to tell you not to come in. But then I realized I didn't have your number."

"Is this morning a bad time?" he asked, looking around at the quiet storefront.

"I talked it over with Lord Nibbles last night and we both decided that I couldn't let you do this. It's too much."

"Who?"

"My guinea pig. The sound of my voice makes him less anxious, so we had a big discussion and I ran everything by him. When I told him I wasn't going to go through with it, he finally relaxed enough to eat the pretzel I was offering him."

"You fed your guinea pig human food? Didn't you hear the story yesterday about the 4-H goat and the cotton candy?"

"It was just one little treat." There was a crease between Vivienne's brows. "You don't think he'll get sick, do you? He looked fine this morning."

Cole tightened his grip on the checkbook. Maybe it was a bad idea to go into business with a woman who took job advice from a rodent. But then again, it wasn't really as if she was actually going to be working for him. The money was just to keep her doing what she was already doing for his brother and Lydia.

Yet before either one of them could persuade the other, a late-model Cadillac sedan pulled diagonally into the two parking spots to the right of his. The older woman's caked-on lipstick was clamped tightly around a cigarette and the rest of her makeup and teased blond hair appeared to have been plastered into place the decade before. Her petite frame and lavender business suit did nothing to detract from her assertiveness as she swung her heavy door open, narrowly missing banging his passenger side.

"Are you that cowboy who was here a few days ago picking up some tables?" The woman's voice sounded just as loud and abrasive as it had when she'd been laying into Vivienne over the phone yesterday.

"I believe that was my brother, ma'am. I'm Cole Dalton." He tipped the brim of his more formal black felt Stetson—after all, nobody could say he hadn't come dressed to take this appointment seriously.

She studied him from under lids weighted down with eye shadow before dropping her cigarette onto the asphalt and stepping on it with a white high-top sneaker that contradicted the rest of her outfit. "I'm guessing you brought the tables back, then?"

"No, Estelle, he's not—" Vivienne started, but Cole cut her off.

He held up his checkbook. "I'm here to book a wedding planner."

The woman's expression went from doubt to dollar signs as she reached out her bony, age-spotted fingers. "Then glad to meet you. Come on inside and Vivienne will get you all squared away with the paperwork."

Estelle didn't release his hand and Cole was forced to follow her as she dragged him past Vivienne and through the door. He pretended not to see the warning look the younger woman directed his way. After five minutes in her boss's company, he knew he made the right choice to offer his help.

The owner of Estelle's Events had the disposition of a yappy Chihuahua and the tenacity of a pit bull.

"But how do you know your fiancée wouldn't go for a hot-air balloon ceremony? If she were here, I would tell her that they're all the rage right now." That was the eighth time Estelle had made a reference to the fact that the so-called bride-to-be wasn't here.

"She's afraid of heights," Cole said, rubbing the bridge of his nose to make sure it wasn't growing.

"Uh-huh," Estelle replied as she slid a colorful brochure across the conference table toward him. "Have her look this over. Just in case."

Cole smiled stiffly as he tucked the folded paper into his front shirt pocket. He looked at Vivienne, who was sitting across from him, hiding behind her laptop screen, her fingers not making any sort of clicking sound on the keyboard.

"How's that contract going?" her boss asked her.

"Um, all I…uh…need is the bride's name." Her eyes pleaded with him to forget this whole thing.

But Estelle looked at him expectantly and Cole knew what would happen if he walked out and Vivienne didn't secure her booking. He said the first name that popped into his mind.

"Susie Starlight." Then, because it sounded way too far-fetched saying it out loud like that, he quickly added, "Roper. Her last name's Roper."

"You've got to be kidding me." Vivienne's face flew up from where she'd been ducking for cover. Her boss made a sound as though she was trying to clear her throat, which ended up triggering a lung-rattling smoker's cough.

"Or Susan, if you want to be formal," Cole said with a purposeful shrug of his shoulders to make his slip seem more plausible. "But everyone calls her by her nickname. Can I get you some water, Estelle?"

The older woman waved him off as she walked back to her office, her wheeze barely subsiding.

"I am not writing that name on a legally binding contract," Vivienne whispered.

"Why does it have to be on there at all? Clearly, I'm the only one who is here to sign the document anyway."

Vivienne studied him across the table. "Estelle probably won't make too much of a fuss about it as long as she gets her deposit."

She tapped the keys a few times and gave the mouse a click, and the printer in the corner whirred to life just as her boss walked back in, sucking on a lollipop. "I've been trying to cut back on the nicotine," Estelle said around the white stick. "Viv got me these to help take the edge off."

"Sounds like Viv here is quite the asset," Cole suggested, but the asset in question made a subtle sweeping gesture across her neck. Yeah, maybe he was laying it on too thick. Already uncomfortable with the false details he was making up to just keep this big lie believable, he shifted in his seat and said, "Who do I make the check out to?"

Estelle eagerly took the twenty-five percent down payment of the company's fee, her sneakers squeaking across the hardwood floor as she hotfooted it back to her office—probably to make out the bank deposit slip. He wouldn't be surprised if the ol' gal didn't have one of those apps on her phone that snapped a picture of the check to transfer the funds before he changed his mind.

Cole looked over the paperwork, then lowered his voice. "I hope you stipulated in here that I'd be working primarily with you."

"Don't worry. Estelle doesn't bother leaving the office much these days. Besides the occasional phone call, I'm almost always the one who works with the clients." Vivienne handed him a contact information form to fill out. "But she will want the bride's email address to register her for a subscription service from various wedding vendors. I suggest you give her yours unless you want them kicked back as invalid."

Cole wrote down his contact information, wishing he had thought this whole plan out a little better. Or at least wishing he hadn't underestimated Vivienne's boss.

"Here's your detail organizer, Mr. Dalton," Estelle said as she brought a large three-ring binder into the room. He recognized it as the same type Vivienne brought to all her meetings with Lydia and Zach. The company must buy them in bulk. "Why don't you and Vivienne get started on filling it in with ideas?"

"Actually, I'm starved." Cole leaned back and patted his stomach. It was a bit early for lunch, but trying to outmaneuver a crafty businesswoman had certainly worked up an appetite. Plus, he couldn't take sitting in this office a second longer. "Vivienne, is there someplace nearby where we can grab a bite and go over this stuff?"

"Of course there is," Estelle responded on Vivienne's behalf, making a shooing gesture at them. "Go on now, Viv. Give the client what they want. That's our motto here."

Vivienne's mouth opened as if to object, probably because her boss had just spent the entire meeting trying to convince Cole of things he absolutely did *not* want.

Ever.

In fact, right this second, the only things he wanted were a good meal and the satisfaction from doing a good deed. He was about to get both.

"Susie Starlight?" was the first thing out of Vivienne's mouth when they sat down at Matilda's Diner and Pie Shop. The only reason she'd agreed to join him for lunch was because she'd been eager to get out from under Estelle's watchful eye and remind Cole that what they were doing was a horrible idea. She certainly hadn't intended to bring up his fictitious fiancée.

"That was the name of my first love." Cole didn't bother looking up as he casually read his menu. Not that this was a date or anything, but their newly formed business arrangement didn't lessen the stab of jealousy Vivienne experienced. Or maybe it was irritation that she was out in public with a man who was still pining over another woman.

"Was she a showgirl?"

"No. She was my horse. I hardly think someone who refers to their guinea pig as Lord Nibbles should talk."

"Well, he didn't start out as *mine*," Vivienne said before thanking the server who delivered two iced waters.

"I've gotta hear this," Cole said, raising one dark eyebrow as if he was actually interested in talking about her pet.

Vivienne sighed and sat back against the leather booth. As long as she didn't have to talk about her boss or getting fired from her job, the man could lead the conversation in any direction he wanted. "He was Estelle's. I don't know what she was thinking when she up and bought him a few weeks ago. I was supposed to return him to the pet store, but I kept finding reasons not to."

"Such as…?"

"Such as he's absolutely adorable whenever I feed him and he daintily starts nibbling on his morsels, as though he is at a proper dinner party."

"Okay, so that explains the 'Nibbles' part of the name," Cole replied, then stood up to retrieve a red crayon that had rolled off the table next to them. He handed it to the toddler in the high chair before sliding back into their booth and not missing a beat of their conversation. "But why 'Lord'?"

"Because he's very proper, like a British peer. And he has this black fur with a funny patch of white on his chest that makes him look like he's wearing a waistcoat."

Vivienne pretended to look for the waitress so she wouldn't have to see Cole laughing at her. Clearly she'd been reading too many Regency romance novels lately.

The restaurant was busy, but the server was quick to return to their table. Cole ordered the grilled chicken club and was polite enough not to say anything when Vivienne requested a hot pastrami sandwich, loaded tater tots and a slice of cookies-and-cream pie.

"I eat when I'm stressed," she said by way of explanation.

"Why are you stressed?" he asked. "You got your booking and Estelle got her check. You're off the hook, aren't you?"

"Ha. You don't know Estelle if you think she's ever going to be appeased." Vivienne pulled the brand-new three-ring binder out of her tote bag and set it down on the table between them. "She'll get suspicious if I bring this thing back empty. The real work is about to start."

## *Chapter Seven*

Cole fingered the indexed tabs of the binder, handling it as though it was a live explosive. "Do you seriously fill one of these things up with info on every single wedding?"

"Usually it's just for ideas. And I prefer to keep things organized on my tablet. But Estelle is still wrestling with the age of technology and likes to be able to monitor my work. Plus, you never know when you're going to be out of Wi-Fi reception or lose power." Vivienne didn't point out that she'd had low signals on both when she'd been working on their property in Rust Creek Falls.

"So how much is my pretend wedding going to cost?" He stared at the list on the first page and did a double take when his eyes landed on the suggested budget. "Whoa. Do people seriously pay this much for a party?"

Vivienne gave her shoulder a slight lift. "Some people do."

"Would you?" The question caught her off guard. People always asked her opinion on what *they* should do. But they never asked her what *she* would do. The truth was she didn't know.

"Probably not. But I'm not your normal bride."

"Do you want to be one someday?"

"I'm not going to say that I haven't thought about it. But I've also thought about whether or not to cut my hair short."

"Don't. I like it long."

A shiver raced down her spine, and she kept her hands clamped together in her lap so she wouldn't be tempted to self-consciously tug on her loose ponytail. "I, uh, was just making a comparison on how it's one of those things that crosses your mind, but you don't actively consider it because, deep down, you don't really have any intention of making any changes."

He studied her so intently she wondered if she'd spoken a different language. Then he said, "Usually when a good idea crosses my mind, I make it happen."

"As is evident by you showing up at my office this morning," she murmured. Then she spoke louder, "Do you always rush into things like this?"

"You mean into helping people when they need me? Of course."

One of Zach's comments the first day they'd met

kept coming back to Vivienne. What was it? Something about being a hero?

"So what did your family say about you rushing into this?" Vivienne tapped lightly on the binder. He was temporarily saved from responding by the appearance of their lunch.

The server had plates arranged up her extended arm as she set food down in front of them. Way too much food. Even stressed, Vivienne didn't think she could eat this much.

"Here's the thing," Cole said after blowing on one of his French fries. "I didn't say anything to them yet. Do you think your boss will tell my brother and Lydia what we're up to?"

*"We?"* She had tried to talk Cole out of this stupid farce, but at this point the ball was already rolling with no way to stop it. Making her just as culpable. She took a sip of her soda before continuing. "Most likely not. Up until now, I've kept Estelle out of the loop with their wedding by scheduling appointments either in Rust Creek Falls or when she's out of the office. Which I would've had you do as well, if you hadn't just shown up out of the blue like that this morning."

"It wasn't out of the blue. I told you I was coming. Are you going to eat all those tater tots?"

Vivienne put the side dish in the middle of the table, right on top of the binder, so he could reach them. "Yeah, but I'd figured you'd change your mind when you realized that it was a stupid idea. I was up half the night thinking of ways to talk you out of it."

"Well, apparently my idea worked, so it wasn't that

stupid. Estelle bought it. Which means you still have a job and my brother still has a wedding planner."

"For now. But if I go back to the office without your ideas on guest counts, indoor venues and favorite cake flavors, she's going to know something's up. I'm telling you, the woman is ruthless."

"Come on." Cole took a long gulp of his iced tea, the smooth muscles of his neck flexing as he swallowed. "I was a Marine. I think I can handle a little old lady in a purple suit."

Famous last words.

Cole hadn't expected Estelle of Estelle's Events to blow up his email inbox with so many links to bridal services. Hell, he didn't even know there were this many bridal services out there. But since they'd gotten along pretty well at lunch and he'd been able to control himself from kissing her, he pulled out Vivienne's business card that evening and sent her a one-word text message: Help.

As soon as he'd pressed the send button, he'd wanted to call it back. Cole wasn't the one usually asking for assistance. He was the one delivering it. But it was well after business hours and he was afraid that if he didn't send something requiring an instant response, he'd spend the rest of the evening wondering if she was avoiding him.

He had to wait only half a minute before she replied: What's wrong?

Cole leaned against the pillows on his bed—which was really his cousin Kayla's old bed—and typed.

I keep getting these emails about laser hair removal and spray-on tans that won't stain my white dress. Am I supposed to respond to Estelle every time she sends me one of these?

Please don't. It will only encourage her.

Then she sent a separate message with just a smiley face.

He chuckled, then tapped his screen. Did she like my answers to the questionnaire?

There'd been an initial interview form Vivienne had gone over with him at lunch. She'd cautioned him about his tongue-in-cheek responses, but he'd made her laugh with a few of them and he was pleased to see that the woman had a great sense of humor.

Suffice it to say she wasn't a fan of the hay bale racing idea or your preference for the groomsmen to wear cow-printed vests.

A second bubble popped up.

She also said she hopes Susie Starlight Roper has more sense than you. I told her not to hold her breath.

A pang of nostalgia shot through Cole at the reminder of his childhood mare. What he'd said earlier today was true. Old Susie had been his first love, but he had no idea why he'd come up with her name when asked about his fake bride. Maybe because all the wedding business and planning for the new ranch had him constantly thinking about their old home in Hardin, as well as his mother and the life he no longer had.

Another alert popped up on the blue envelope app, which he normally never used, since he mostly worked with horses and cows and they never sent him emails. He clicked on the link, only to get the annoying little red alert symbol to disappear. Cole groaned at the subject line and then sent Vivienne another text.

Do you know they have stores where you can go online and pick out which gifts you want people to give you for a wedding present?

They're called wedding registries. But don't worry. You and Susie won't need to start one until right before you send out your invitations.

Ol' Susie would've been happy registering for a new saddle blanket and a bag of carrots.

That means 2 of your guests will be buying a gift. What should the other 498 people related to you bring?

Cole smiled to himself as he reread her joke about his large family. He wanted to write back something clever, but everything he could think of might come across as too flirtatious.

Nothing. I still can't believe people waste their money on this junk.

I know. You should've seen this one client we had today. That sucker paid us money up front to plan a fake wedding for him.

Cole was still laughing when he set his phone down and switched off the pink lamp on the bedside table.

But he wasn't laughing two days later when, after a hot, backbreaking day of digging around railroad ties and laying cement for Vivienne's walkway, he made the mistake of looking at his inbox right before bed. The advertisement about bridal lingerie had him tossing and turning all night, thinking about Vivienne dressed in nothing but a white, lacy bustier…and his desire to get her out of it as fast as possible!

Vivienne was having some fantasies of her own, and they weren't all about resurrecting her career. It didn't help that, in order to keep up pretenses, she'd had to call several times this week to ask Cole things like his preference for a DJ over a band and whether his "fiancée" would be interested in a special promotion the bowling alley in Kalispell was having for bridal showers and bachelorette parties.

Estelle wasn't letting up, despite the fact that Vivienne had a consultation scheduled for the anniversary party of a former client's parents, as well as several leads on more events.

Then, the following Monday, Cole sent her a text jokingly asking where he should go on his honeymoon. She was on the home stretch on the Grant-Dalton wedding while trying to convince her boss that she was still working on more bookings, and all she could think about was Cole walking on a beach on the French Riviera, dripping water off his rippling muscles and—

Whoa. She really should not be going there.

Thankfully, Estelle's late arrival was a welcome distraction from Vivienne's inappropriate thoughts. The older woman hustled through the front door of the office with more agility than an Olympic runner.

"Where are we with the Roper-Dalton wedding?"

Okay, maybe that wasn't quite the distraction Vivienne had been hoping for. "We're right where we need to be on it."

"Have they set a date yet?"

"Last I heard, the groom wanted to focus on his brother's event before starting the planning of his own."

"That's odd, if you ask me." Estelle dropped her purple handbag on the reception desk, where it would probably remain until Vivienne moved it.

"I think it's pretty normal that someone wouldn't want to upstage their sibling on their big day."

Estelle shooed a hand at her. "Not that. I mean, it's odd that we're still only dealing with the groom. What kind of bride doesn't take an active role in the planning of her own wedding?"

"It's still early. I'm sure Su—" Vivienne couldn't bring herself to finish the fake name. "I'm sure the bride will make an appearance soon."

Vivienne realized the odd choice of words when Estelle paused halfway down the hall toward her office. Oh, no. Her boss turned around. "Actually, why don't you call her and ask when she's coming into the office to sign the contract?"

Yeah, she'd been wrong about Estelle not wanting both of their clients' signatures. Why have only one person on the hook for a cancellation fee when she could have two? Vivienne should've never second-guessed the woman's dogged tenacity when it involved the risk of forfeited deposits.

"No problem." What could she do but paste a smile on her face as if there was nothing she'd enjoy more than making a pretend phone call to a pretend bride. Vivienne's veins felt as if they were pumping ice water, and she looked at the thermostat on the wall to see if the air-conditioning had been switched on. She tried to keep her teeth from chattering when she offered a weak excuse. "Except I only have the number for the groom."

"Then call him," Estelle said, pulling out one of the heavy chairs across the conference table and settling her tiny frame in the middle of it, a queen on her throne.

Vivienne opened the binder and flipped to the client information sheet. After all, she didn't need her boss to know she already had Cole's number programmed in her contact list or that they'd been talking to each other all week. When she pulled out her cell phone to dial, Estelle tapped a long, purple fingernail on the black landline, indicating she wanted the call on speaker.

Each drawn-out ring echoed in the conference room and grated on Vivienne's tightly wound nerves. Just when she thought the call was about to go to voice mail, Cole's sexy drawl answered.

"Hi, Cole, this is Vivienne Shuster from Estelle's Events."

"Oh, hey. Why are you calling me from a different—"

"I'm here with Estelle and we have you on speaker."

Cole cleared his throat. "What can I do for you ladies?"

"This is Estelle speaking." Her boss's voice was deeper and raspier, and since she was yelling directly into the desk phone, it was also louder than Vivienne's. She rolled her eyes at the unnecessary introduction, but Estelle continued. "I wanted to know when your fiancée is going to be coming into the office to sign the contract."

There was a long pause on the other end of the line before Cole finally spoke up. "Well, you see, ma'am, my fiancée lives in Billings and she doesn't get much time off from her job."

"What does she do again for work?" Estelle asked, leading him down a path that might prove to be too slippery.

"She's a model."

"In Billings?" Her boss looked doubtful.

"Yep. Definitely in Billings. There's a big demand over there for ads with feed companies and horse shows. You know, that sort of thing." The lies rolled off the man's tongue so easily, Vivienne began to wonder if he'd carefully prepared his answers or if he actually believed everything he was saying.

"Billings, you say?" Or maybe Estelle wasn't all there mentally, because the man had said the city's name twice already. Then Vivienne saw the gleam in her boss's eye and her blood went from cold to frozen when Estelle covered the speaker and whispered, "She might have more model friends. That's a much bigger market for us to get into."

Vivienne wanted to yank the phone cord from the wall. She wanted to scream out a warning to Cole. But there was no stopping Estelle, who removed her hand from the speaker and kept talking.

"What a coincidence. There's a bridal expo going on in Billings and I was going to send Vivienne," the woman said, causing Vivienne's head to jerk up because this was news to her. "Cole, why don't you drive on over there, as well? Viv can take you and Susie to the event. We have lots of contacts out that way and you might even find a venue more suitable for someone in the modeling industry."

Vivienne reached into her go bag for her emergency stash of chocolate.

"I…uh…" Cole started, but he was having a difficult time coming up with a diplomatic way to tell the older woman what he was really thinking.

"That wouldn't be a problem for you, would it?" Estelle's raspy voice taunted.

*In for a penny, in for a pound*, his mom used to always tell her sons when they committed to something. While Cole doubted that his mother would've approved of his less-than-honest methods, she would've been glad that he was doing this for Zach. "I think I can swing that."

Cole made up an excuse about a cow getting loose from the herd—even though he was currently in his truck in the parking lot at the hardware store in the middle of Rust Creek Falls, where there wasn't a heifer to be found—and quickly disconnected. He needed to get his breathing under control and rethink his moral downfall before the owner of Estelle's Events roped him into any more ridiculous lies.

Less than an hour later, just when he'd thought of a legitimate reason he couldn't go on the trip to Billings, his phone rang again. This time, Vivienne's cell was the number that popped up on his screen. Still, he answered tentatively just in case he was on speaker again.

"Why did Susie Starlight have to be a model living in Billings?" she asked by way of greeting, indicating that nobody else was within listening distance.

"Because I was trying to stick to the truth as much as possible. When I was eleven, my mom had a photographer friend who needed a white horse in Billings to do some photo shoots for a grain company there. I didn't get to go because I couldn't miss school. I missed her like crazy."

"You know that you're not actually planning a wedding with your childhood horse, right?"

"I'm not supposed to be planning a wedding with anyone. But here we are."

Vivienne groaned. "Estelle's already registered me for the expo and ordered new company brochures and business cards for me to pass out while we're there. Thank goodness she finally left for her hair appointment, but not before she warned me that Rich LaRue is also going to be there. God forbid the man gets to one of our potential clients first."

"Who?"

"He owns another event planning company called A LaVish Affair. He's Estelle's biggest competitor and her sworn nemesis. I'm not sure, but I think there might be a court order somewhere directing Estelle not to get within five hundred feet of him, which is why she obviously can't go herself."

"You should look on the bright side, then. At least you'll get a free trip to Billings and a weekend away from your nightmare of a boss."

"Ugh. I don't have an extra weekend like this to waste. Do you have any idea how much I still need to do for Zach and Lydia's wedding? Wait, did you just say *you*?"

"Uh…" Cole had no idea where the woman was going with this rant. "What?"

"You did. You said *you*. As in *I'll* get a free trip to Billings. *I'll* be going alone."

Cole tossed his hat onto the bench seat of the truck so he could scratch his forehead. "I'm confused. Are you not going?"

"Oh, I'm going all right. But you're the one who decided to have a fiancée over there. So if I have to go to Billings, you're coming with me."

## Chapter Eight

The sun had yet to rise on Saturday morning when Vivienne gave Lord Nibbles an extra scoop of food and a handful of grapes. "This should hold you over until tomorrow. Be good while I'm gone."

Her one-bedroom apartment had come furnished, and despite her love of fashion and decorating and entertaining, Vivienne had never done much to spruce the place up. When she'd been growing up, one of her parents had moved out so often that personal effects had become a symbol of petty property disputes, such as who got to take the brand-new comforter set and who had to make do with the odd-shaped quilt her great-aunt Shelly had sewn for their wedding gift. Neither her mom nor her dad had wanted either; they just wanted to argue over the items.

The last thing she wanted was for Cole to see her lackluster homemaking skills and get the impression that she wasn't up to the task of beautifying his family's property in time for the wedding. It would be better to simply meet him outside.

She was loading her small carry-on suitcase into the trunk of the Jetta just as Cole's truck pulled into her apartment lot. Billings was almost a seven-hour drive, so there was no point in them taking separate cars. Besides, the man had offered to do most of the driving, which would free Vivienne up to make last-minute phone calls to vendors and to track down a railway handcart, which she'd promised to Garrett.

It also freed her up from having to wonder if Cole would be staring at her, because the man couldn't possibly pay attention to her if he had to keep his eyes on the road. Hopefully.

"What time are we supposed to be there?" he asked, stifling a yawn.

"Not until one. Luckily, Estelle was too late to register for a booth, so we're going to be free to walk around and check out everyone else's exhibits."

"And pass out brochures to get you more customers." Cole took the keys from her hand. "I mean, that's why you're going in the first place, right?"

"Something like that," she replied, before thanking him for holding open the passenger door for her. When he scrunched his six-foot frame into the driver's seat without complaint, she realized that they both needed to make the most of this awkward situation. "I know I'm supposed to be networking and finding more business, but it just doesn't feel very organic to walk up to strangers out of the blue and hand them my business card."

"That makes sense." He started the car and said, "When we get there, give me a stack and I'll help. The sooner we hand them out, the sooner we can get out of that place. I had nightmares the past two nights about some overeager bride mistaking me for her groom and tricking me into exchanging vows with her."

"You know it doesn't work like that, right?" she asked as Cole pulled out of the parking lot. Even though the road was deserted this early in the morning, he used his turn indicator and kept under the speed limit. This guy drove the same way he handled any other responsibility, like it was the most important task he'd ever been assigned.

"How does it work?"

"You have to get an actual marriage license at a county courthouse. You go there in person, show your ID and sign for it. *Then* you get mistaken for a willing groom and tricked into a ceremony. Since it's Saturday and all the county offices are likely closed, you shouldn't be able to get yourself into too much trouble."

"That's a relief."

"But I think it's cute that you're under the impression women you don't know are going to be falling over themselves trying to trick you into marriage."

"I didn't say falling over themselves, but some women find me—"

The ringing of her cell phone interrupted what he was going to say and Vivienne found herself suddenly curious about what some women found. Her bubble of curiosity popped, though, when she saw who was calling her at this hour.

"Hi, Mom. Is everything okay?"

"I'm leaving him," came Bonnie Shuster's reply. "I thought things would be different this time, but your father will never change."

"You always think it will be different," Vivienne said. She covered up the mouthpiece and whispered to Cole, "Excuse me for a minute."

"Do you know where he is right this second?" her mother asked, but the question was clearly rhetorical. Anyone who'd had a front row seat to the dysfunctional relationship of Bonnie and Richard Shuster could easily guess where her father was.

"At his apartment?" Vivienne asked at the same time her mother announced, "At his apartment."

"Probably with one of his honeys," Bonnie added.

As her mom launched into her version of their recent separation, Vivienne gave the required uh-huhs and murmurs of sympathy. After all, she was an expert at providing them to her parents. A tone for call-waiting beeped and she rolled her eyes, knowing exactly who it was without needing to check the screen.

"Mom, I'm on the road and the reception isn't great. Call me when Dad comes home."

"Mark my words, he is *not* coming home this time," she started, but Vivienne clicked over.

"Hi, Dad."

"Did your mother tell you what she did?" her father asked, before delivering his side of the story, which, as usual, involved a horrible argument over a forgotten anniversary—although, in his defense, who could remember which one to celebrate this year—followed by her mother's accusations of imagined infidelities. Again, she gave the required responses as she only partially listened, trying to get the call over with as quickly as possible.

By the time she disconnected, the sun was lighting up the sky. "Sorry about that."

"Should we turn around?" Cole asked.

"Why?"

"I…uh…couldn't help overhearing, but it sounds like your parents are splitting up."

"They're fine. By this time next week, they'll probably be back together," she said. At his questioning look, she continued. "I know it seems odd. But it's just what they do. Every few months they have some sort of major breakup and declare things are over. Twice, they've even filed for divorce. But then they make up and get back together. They've been married three times. To each other. Not counting all the vow renewals in between."

"That sounds…" Cole didn't finish his thought and she couldn't blame him.

"I know. It's crazy. But, on the bright side, it's also how I landed this job. My parents hired Estelle for one of their vow renewals a few years ago. I was fresh out of college and needed to work somewhere and I was already an expert at planning their so-called celebrations of commitment by that time. So it's been a good fit."

"Yeah, but after growing up that way, how can you

still believe in any of it? I would think you'd be pretty jaded by now." His tone echoed her own skepticism.

"Sometimes I am. But then I'll meet a couple like your brother and Lydia, and they're the kind of people who make it all worth it."

"But there have got to be times when you're planning someone's wedding and you just know for sure that it's never going to last. How do you deal with it?"

Vivienne reached for her sunglasses and slid them onto her eyes, carefully slipping back into professional mode. "I tell myself that I'm giving people what they want."

"Which is a bad marriage?"

"Which is a fairy-tale day. That, I can always deliver. What comes after that day is up to them."

Cole pulled into a McDonald's off the highway so they could use the restrooms and pick up some breakfast sandwiches for the rest of the drive. When they got back on the road, Vivienne asked, "What about you?"

"What about me?"

"What are your thoughts on marriage?" Vivienne's question caught him off guard and he accidentally swallowed a bite of hash brown without chewing it. After he recovered from a coughing fit, she clarified, "I meant, since we're going to a bridal expo, it seems only fitting that as your hired wedding planner, I steer you in the right direction while we're there."

Cole's thoughts on weddings were completely different than his thoughts on marriage. His parents had had a great union, so he knew they were possible. With a lot of work. They were also extremely risky when someone allowed himself to love too much. He took a sip of his coffee before purposely giving a vague response. "I think we all know how I feel about weddings."

"Yep." She powered up her iPad on her lap and began tapping. "But don't worry. There will likely be at least a couple other reluctant guys like you at the convention center in Billings who think everyone else there is nuts."

Several hours and a few hundred miles later, as much as Cole thought he was going to hate the bridal expo, he was actually having a lot of fun. Of course, it helped that when they arrived, the people at the welcome desk didn't have Vivienne's registration as a professional planner on file because of the late registration and they'd had to buy regular passes for the event, complete with name-badge stickers that read Bride and Groom.

Vivienne began to protest, but he'd peeled the thing from its backing and planted it on the neckline of her dress, right above the area that he really wished he could touch. Then he yanked his hand back and cleared his head before sticking on his own.

"Just go with it," he'd told her, and they'd spent the first hour pretending to be an actual couple planning their own wedding. At least it had started out as a good-humored game of pretense, but his palm was still tingling from where he'd touched her under the name tag.

When they were standing in front of samples of wedding cake, he asked, "Did you try the red velvet yet?"

"We've already eaten one from every tray," she whispered back to him. "If you take any more, the baker is going to ask us for a security deposit."

To get her to stop worrying, he took a small square of

cream-cheese-frosted cake and shoved it in her mouth.
But instead of the playful act he'd intended it to be, her
tongue darted out and touched his fingers and Vivienne
closed her eyes, releasing a soft moan.

His pulse spiked to life and a sudden need hummed
through him. Swing music blasted from a DJ's speakers nearby, filtering through his thoughts and reminding him that this was not the time or the place to be
getting aroused.

"Oh, look," he said, making her lashes flutter open.
He stepped behind her and placed his hands on either
side of her waist, steering her toward a booth across
the way. "They have one of those wheels we can spin
to get a prize."

The posters hanging from the freestanding dividers
behind the wheel advertised a luxury spa near Bozeman.

"Those things aren't real prizes, you know," she said.
"They're just gimmicks to get you over to their resort
so that you'll book your reception there."

"You're such a cynic. Just give it a whirl."

Vivienne gave him a doubting look as she took a turn
spinning the wheel. But when she won a box of fancy
chocolate truffles, she jumped up and down as though
she'd just won a free supply of steaks for a year. Her
enthusiasm was infectious and he found himself wrapping his arms around her waist when she bounced a
little too close to him.

She responded by throwing her own arms around
his neck and planting a kiss on his cheek before saying, "I've never won anything before!"

He was quick to release her, but the damage was already done. His skin was on fire and it felt as if her lips had left a brand above his jawline. Vivienne, thankfully, didn't notice because she was clapping her hands as they showed her the two-pound box of chocolate. Cole was still rubbing the affected spot on the side of his face when she grabbed his arm and pushed him toward the wheel. "Now you try."

"Honey," he said loud enough for the representative to hear. "I'm sure they only give out one prize per couple."

His use of the endearment had the desired effect, even if he kicked himself for causing her smile to slip. But the man behind the wheel waved him off and said, "Go ahead, give it a spin."

Not wanting to disappoint his so-called bride, Cole channeled all of his building attraction and tension and spun the wheel so hard it almost flew off the stand. Watching the bright colors go round in such a fast circle made him dizzy and he had to look away, but not before Vivienne grabbed onto his hand and squeezed it in excitement. He didn't look back until the clicking sound slowed, and even then all he could think about were their clasped fingers. Vivienne bounced in triumph again but stilled as soon as the representative asked, "Now, when would you two like to book your free couples massages?"

A free *what*?

The air thickened and his boots felt as if they were squeezing his feet into action. Cole had never had a professional massage, but judging by the photo on the glossy brochure, it involved candles, rose petals and getting naked under a sheet.

Vivienne's cheeks were stained crimson, and when Cole took the clipboard to fill out his contact information, he noticed the blush had spread down her neck and below the V-neck of her dress. His fingers shook slightly as he wrote down his name and number, but luckily Vivienne didn't see because she was too busy walking toward the next booth, her box of chocolates tucked under her arm.

Cole handed the clipboard back to the spa employee, who promised to be in contact. Crap. Why hadn't he given them a bogus email address? The last thing he needed was to be reminded of the awkward fantasy of getting Vivienne on a massage table.

Unfortunately, the next vendor booth was for a travel company, and as Cole approached his "bride," an eager middle-aged woman was midpitch about all the fabulous honeymoon destinations they offered. The agent turned toward him and gestured toward Vivienne. "If you could spend the most romantic week of your life with this lovely lady, where would it be?"

His throat muscles flexed and he had to remind himself how to gulp in more oxygen. At this exact second, the answer to that question was the nearest motel room. But Cole was saved from stuttering out an answer when he spotted a man down the aisle using a wobbly ladder to secure a fallen banner.

"I'll be right back," he said before rushing off. When he got to the man, the first thing Cole did was hold the ladder steady. "Can I give you a hand?"

"Thank you, young man." The gentleman's shiny bald head was a shade of dark mahogany and the silver of his thin mustache suggested his advanced years. He was dressed impeccably in a gray, pin-striped suit with a bright pink handkerchief square poking out his breast pocket. Instead of descending the ladder, though, he finished yanking a zip tie through one of the grommets.

Cole would've preferred the elderly man come down and let him climb the rickety ladder instead. But he didn't want to insult the man's pride. When the hot-pink sign, which matched the man's handkerchief, was finally in place, it read A LaVish Affair and Cole racked his brain for where he'd heard of that name before.

Stepping to the side as the man came down the last few rungs, Cole was surprised to see Vivienne nearby.

"If it isn't Vivienne Shuster." The dapper gentleman beamed a bright white smile before looking over each shoulder. "I don't feel any fire breathing down my neck, so I'm assuming that dragon of a boss of yours isn't with you."

Vivienne wagged a finger before stepping forward and giving the man a kiss on his cheek. She turned to Cole. "May I introduce the famous Rich LaRue of A LaVish Affair."

Cole extended his hand to Rich. He'd known he'd heard the name somewhere. Vivienne was certainly chummy with the guy who was supposedly her company's biggest competitor. "Nice to meet you."

Rich returned the handshake, his rich brown eyes darting between Vivienne's and Cole's name tags. "Looks like congratulations are in order."

"No, no, no!" Vivienne's hand slapped against her chest, covering up her sticker. "You know me, Rich. Always the wedding planner, never the bride."

The man's silver eyebrows lifted.

"Estelle wanted me to attend, but it was a last-minute thing and she was too late to get vendor status, so my *friend* Cole volunteered to come with me and the people at the door just assumed we were a couple and, well…" While Vivienne's explanation trailed off, Rich's forehead remained creased. And a knot formed in Cole's stomach at her emphasis of the word *friend*.

"The only part of that story that makes any sense is Estelle doing something last minute. Darling," Rich called over to an older woman in a frothy pink dress, also color coordinated with their booth. "Vivienne Shuster is here, and I'm pretty sure she's working as an undercover bride to get a different view of the industry. Brilliant strategy. Just brilliant."

"Hi, Glory," Vivienne smiled and waved at the lady who must be Rich's wife. "I'm not really undercover."

Rich leaned in toward Cole. "I've been telling her for years that she's wasting her talents working for Estelle."

Cole had only seen her in action with one wedding— not counting his own—and had already deduced that for himself.

Vivienne chuckled and patted Rich's hand. "You flatter me when you have potential clients you should be flattering instead."

"Time to get back to work." Rich straightened his lapels, then winked at Vivienne before stage-whispering, "And, don't worry. I won't blow your cover."

As they walked away, Cole tried to stick by Vivienne's side as she navigated them through a herd of ladies decked out in bridal gowns. A veil whipped at his face, catching him in the eye, and he lost sight of her for a second. But then her warm, strong hand clamped onto his and he held on for dear life as she pulled him to safety.

"Don't worry," she said as they moved into a booth occupied by an empty dentist chair and a sign advertising that Dr. Smile was the leading orthodontist in Billings. Vivienne squeezed his arm. "Your nightmare isn't coming true. You're not in danger of being forced to marry one of them."

Cole grinned at the reference, and not just because he wanted Dr. Smile to see that he didn't need braces before his upcoming wedding. This morning, when he'd told her about that, he'd said the word *nightmare*, but it really had been just a dream. It had even been a pleasant one where he was standing at the altar, excited to see an unknown bride walking down the aisle toward him. He'd startled awake before he'd figured out her identity, and the uncertainty of what the dream might mean had prevented him from going back to sleep. He nodded toward the mass of women moving toward the rear of the convention center like a cluster of fluffy white clouds. "Why are they in costume?"

"Because the fashion show is getting ready to start."

He couldn't stop from cringing. "Please tell me we can skip that part of the expo."

"Why? They're also going to be showing tons of bridesmaid dresses and all the latest flower-girl accessories."

Cole forced a chuckle, hoping she would join in. When she didn't, he said, "You know, you do a really good job of keeping a straight face when you're teasing."

"Who says I'm teasing?"

## Chapter Nine

Most of the vendors were taking down their booths by the time Vivienne passed out only her fifth business card of the day. And it was to a florist out of Whitefish, not even a potential client. But the expo hadn't been a total waste. She'd gotten plenty of ideas and had actually enjoyed getting to play the bride for a change. A cosmetician providing complimentary makeup consultations even applied a set of fake lashes when Vivienne had a beauty makeover.

"I'm starving," Cole said as he hoisted a free canvas tote higher on his shoulder. They had been plied with swag bags and giveaway items every time they'd turned around. "Let's go grab some dinner."

"I don't see how you can be so hungry. I'm pretty sure you hit every catering booth in this place, filling up on samples," Vivienne teased, trying not to bat her long false eyelashes at him.

"C'mon. That wasn't real food. Just little bites here and there. I haven't had anything substantial since breakfast."

As they exited the convention center, Vivienne was relieved to see the sun was barely starting to set. She hadn't intended to stay so long, yet they'd practically closed the place down. Now that the pretense of being a carefree bride was fading away, her appetite was returning. Or, at least, the stress of spending more alone time with Cole was returning.

What she should do was check into the hotel, take a long shower, order some room service and open up the complimentary bottle of wine she'd gotten from a local vineyard that doubled as a wedding venue. Instead, she let Cole and the scent of herbs and sizzling meat guide her to the steakhouse across the street.

Neon lights curved around the arched entrance, and, when Cole opened the door for her, Vivienne didn't know if she was going into a restaurant or a honky-tonk. It soon became obvious that not only was it an eating establishment, it was one in high demand. When the hostess told them that there was a thirty-minute wait for a party of two, Vivienne shrugged and expected Cole to suggest a burger place down the road. He surprised her by saying, "Let's go grab a drink in the bar."

A flush of panic raced through her and she wondered what Cole meant by grabbing a drink. Having dinner with a client, even a pretend one, might arguably count as a business meeting and she could convince herself that she was still well within the bounds of professional behavior. However, sitting in a bar with a single man on a Saturday night had to cross some sort of ethical line.

Before she could think of which line that was, a server passed by with a tray weighted down by plates of prime rib au jus, mashed potatoes and creamed corn. Vivienne's mouth watered and her nose twitched as she followed the food into the depths of the restaurant. Cole caught up to her, and she felt his hand on her lower back steering her toward the lounge instead of the dining area.

The bar was equally crowded, but a high table opened up when another couple stood, hoisting a blinking pager overhead like they'd just won a trophy. Vivienne's stomach growled as she took a seat and Cole handed her a cocktail menu.

"Do you want to split an appetizer?" he asked, right as a woman wearing a motorcycle club vest and a tiara studded with plastic jewels spelling out Fifty and Nifty stood up to take a picture with the rest of the female bikers at the table nearby.

Unfortunately, the woman stumbled and got herself tangled up in a nest of birthday balloons tied to her chair. There was a loud pop, followed by a clinking sound before something thudded, and glass shattered on the ground. Several of the woman's friends—who wore similar leather vests and matching black T-shirts emblazoned with Judy's 50th Birthday Ride—shrieked, and Cole jumped off his high-backed stool and sprang into action. Within seconds, he had Judy untangled and was already kneeling down, picking up shards of a martini glass before the restaurant staff could respond.

A waiter used a damp washcloth to wipe up the spilled drink and Cole went to the bar, returning with a fresh neon-blue cocktail for the embarrassed birthday woman. He even offered to take a picture of the group using her phone.

The women gathered back into position for the photo and Cole counted to three.

"Here." One of Judy's friends handed a camera to the waiter. "Will you get one of us with the sexy cowboy?"

It was hard to tell with the dim interior lighting, but Cole's cheeks had turned a shade pinker. Still, what did the guy expect when he went around town in a cowboy hat and scuffed boots, dressed like a rodeo hunk? Vivienne bit back her laughter when the oldest member of the group patted Cole's rear end as he walked away.

When he returned to their table, Vivienne was still smiling. "Now I know why your family calls you Sergeant Save-the-Day."

Cole's blush actually deepened and he cleared his throat. "Well, then maybe you can explain it, because I have no idea why they do that."

"Really? No idea?" Vivienne made a *pfshh* sound. At Cole's blank look, she continued. "Let's see. Since we only have thirty minutes to kill, I'll limit my examples to today's rescues alone. First there was the mother fussing with her stroller in the registration line. You got the baby blanket unstuck from the wheel for her. Then there were the two girls who were fighting over the flower-girl wands at that florist's booth.

That took some smooth talking, but you bought them both their own crowns. And what about the older guy using a cane and tiring out quickly? You got him one of those motorized scooters available at the entrance and came riding to his rescue, like a cowboy on his trusty, battery-powered steed."

"They needed help."

"Have you ever noticed that you're always in the right place at the right time?"

A frown marred Cole's face for the briefest of moments, but then the harried server who'd just finished cleaning up the mess at the nearby table approached with two electric-blue cocktails in martini glasses. The waiter tilted his head toward the female biker group. "The ladies bought your first round."

Cole's lips turned down and his nose wrinkled at the fruity drinks. But he was too polite to send them back. Instead, he placed both in front of Vivienne and asked the server, "What kind of craft beer do you have on tap?"

After hearing several choices, Cole selected the pale ale. The waiter was in full retreat when Cole said, "Crap, we forgot to order the appetizer."

He handed her the bar menu and asked again if she wanted to split something. "Don't change the subject." She wagged a finger at him. "You were about to tell me why you're always the first one to respond to a crisis."

He groaned, or at least it sounded like a groan. It was becoming more crowded in there and Vivienne had to lean in closer to hear him.

"What was that?"

He scooted his chair up to hers. "I said I was just doing what anyone else would have done."

"No, you weren't. Don't try to be modest." Vivienne took a sip of the blue drink and winced at its sweetness. "You earned that nickname fair and square. And I want to know how."

Another blush spotted his cheeks, right under the shadow of his beard, and since his beer hadn't arrived, he helped himself to the other cocktail. He shuddered, then flicked his tongue out to capture the sugary crystals the rim of his glass had left on his upper lip. Vivienne's own mouth went dry and she took another gulp. But she wasn't going to let her attraction to him distract her. "I'm waiting."

"Fine," he finally relented. "It started the summer I was eight years old. It was a hot one and our parents took us camping at Flathead Lake. When we got there, my dad was busy showing The Bigs how to set up their tents."

"Wait," Vivienne interrupted. "Who are The Bigs?"

"Booker and Garrett. They're the oldest. Anyway, my mom was trying to unload the truck but kept having to chase after The Smalls—that's Zach and Shawn."

"So your family had The Bigs and The Smalls. Which group did you fall into?"

"Neither. I was in the middle, the overlooked kid who didn't really fit into either category. So I was given the boring task of lining rocks around the fire pit, which really was just a stupid chore my parents made up to keep me out of the way. But it also meant that I was the only one paying attention when ten-year-old Garrett was lured away from the campsite by the promise of the cool lake water."

The waiter returned just then with Cole's beer, along with an ice bucket containing a bottle of champagne. Again the server nodded toward the women at the birthday party table, which was getting a bit louder and had been increased with the arrival of four older gentlemen who Vivienne could've sworn had been seated at the bar when they'd arrived. "The ladies also wanted to wish you congratulations."

Cole's brows slammed together and Vivienne would've laughed at his response if she hadn't been equally confused.

"Hey, you two," Judy, in her birthday tiara, yelled across the room. "Good luck on your marriage. Hope it lasts longer than mine did."

The rest of the women cheered and cackled as Vivienne looked down at Cole's chest. Whoops. They were still wearing their Bride and Groom name tags. She managed a guilty smile as she used one hand to give a polite wave and the other hand to discreetly peel the sticker off her dress.

Cole unclenched his jaw long enough to down the rest of the martini. "Whoa, that was sweet," he said before taking a gulp of beer, probably to wash away the sugary taste.

The waiter had already removed the champagne cork, so it wasn't like they could send the bottle back. He brought over two flutes, and Vivienne quickly swallowed the rest of her cocktail so the server could clear the empty glasses and their table didn't resemble a fraternity house the morning after a homecoming party.

"So Garrett wandered off to the lake?"

Cole nodded. "He did. And I followed him, even though we'd all been told repeatedly to stay away from the water. But before I could make it down the embankment, he already had his shoes off and was wading in. I told him he was going to be in big trouble. But did he listen to me? Nope. When it comes to Garrett, everything's got to be faster and more dangerous." Cole finished off his beer. "Jeez, what was in that first drink? Pineapple? I can still taste it."

Vivienne filled both the champagne flutes, just in case he needed something else to drink. The waiter and bartender were being overrun with customers and there was no way they'd get some iced water before they sat down to eat. "So what happened to Garrett?"

"The knucklehead accidentally stepped on a rusted-out fishing hook and sliced open the bottom of his foot."

"Oh, no," Vivienne gasped. She looked at Cole's forearm and wondered how her hand had gotten there. However, her muscles felt too relaxed to pull it away.

"Oh, yes. So he's crying like a baby while I'm shoving his foot into the water trying to clean the wound. I found his discarded sock and tied it around the gash to stop the bleeding, then I carried him almost a quarter of a mile back to camp."

"You carried him? But wasn't he bigger than you?"

"By ten pounds, at least. Afterward, my parents were telling me how proud they were of me—before they yelled at both of us for wandering off. The campground host said I was the bravest boy who'd ever stayed there and the doctor at the urgent-care office praised my quick thinking, right before he gave Garrett a tetanus shot. Suddenly I went from being the forgotten middle child to the kid who saved the day."

"Hence the nickname?" she asked.

"Well, technically it started out as Ranger Rescue, but when I enrolled in ROTC in high school, it got switched to the military-themed version."

The pager lit up and vibrated against her champagne glass. Thank goodness their table was finally ready, because Vivienne's head was feeling lighter and she was having a difficult time backing away from Cole. She needed to get some food in her to soak up the alcohol she'd drunk too quickly. Or else she was bound to do something reckless.

Cole followed behind, his hand again at the small of Vivienne's back as he guided her to the hostess stand. Maybe it was the warming effects of the booze in his bloodstream, but the fabric of her wraparound dress was so thin her heated skin underneath left an imprint on his palm long after they were handed their heavy leather-bound menus.

"I see we already have drinks taken care of," a waitress said before setting down the ice bucket Cole had purposely left behind in the bar area. Usually he wasn't a big drinker, and he definitely didn't mix his alcohol. But since when had any part of this day been normal?

The young woman introduced herself as Heather and rattled off several specials. He'd seen the way Vivienne had been staring at the prime rib earlier and was willing to place a wager on what she'd order. Of course, he'd also seen the way she'd been staring at him, and he wondered how he'd make it through dinner if she leaned in and touched his arm again.

He was already exhausted from the long drive here, plus all the bridal expo nonsense, which was like nothing he'd ever experienced. Overstimulation had the potential to wreak havoc on his common sense when he was sober, so it was no surprise that the liquor was now doing the thinking for him, telling him that the soft knit dress hugging Vivienne's curves couldn't possibly be as smooth as—

"Let's start off with the sampler platter," Vivienne told Heather, snapping him back to reality. "I'd also like the wedge salad with blue cheese dressing and extra bacon bits. And the French onion soup. Oh, and if we could get some bread while we look over the rest of the menu, that'd be great."

"I thought you said we couldn't possibly be hungry after all those samples today," Cole reminded her when the server walked away.

"I know. But now I'm starving. What do you think is better here? The porterhouse or the prime rib?"

He recalled her joke about eating whenever she was stressed and he wondered if that was the case now. But they'd had fun for the most part and she'd been in her element, surrounded by brides and bouquets and beauty products. What could she possibly be stressed about?

Four courses and a bottle of champagne later, Vivienne ordered a slice of chocolate lava cake to go and

Cole slipped his credit card to the waitress. There was a brief argument about who should pay, since it was a business dinner. Yet Cole insisted. "Remember the company motto? I'm the customer, which means I'm always right."

"You're a client, not a customer," Vivienne replied.

"Do you normally polish off a bottle of champagne with your clients?"

"Oh, my gosh, I can't believe we finished the whole thing." She let out a little giggle, then covered her mouth and attempted a serious expression. "But the answer to that is no, I don't."

"I figured as much." Cole stood up and pulled her chair out. He tried not to stare at her rear end as he followed her toward the exit. But he couldn't keep his eyes off her tonight. Hell, who was he kidding? He hadn't been able to keep his eyes off Vivienne Shuster since the day he met her. Walking behind her, watching her hips sway and not being able to put his hands on either side of them and pull her to him was excruciating.

When they finally got outside, she said, "I'm so full you're going to have to roll me over to the hotel."

Cole stopped in the middle of the sidewalk. He'd been overheated in the restaurant and hadn't expected such a temperature drop in the cool evening air. Or perhaps he was frozen at the suggestion of a hotel, which implied they'd be staying here overnight. Together. "What hotel?"

"The one by the convention center."

His heart thumped frantically behind his rib cage. "You...uh...want to get a room?"

"I already have one. Or a reservation at least. I still have to check in, though. As do you."

A pang of disappointment slowed his racing pulse. So she hadn't meant that they'd be sharing a room. Or a bed. But he was still foggy on the part about having a reservation. "I didn't realize we were staying here tonight. But I guess neither one of us is in any shape to drive the seven hours home."

While they weren't falling-down drunk, either, Cole was usually much more prudent about driving after even one beer, let alone two, plus a blue fruity cocktail and half a bottle of champagne. But being with Vivienne made him do things he never would've imagined doing if he had his wits about him. Like attending a bridal expo or pretending to be engaged to get free samples.

He had begun to walk with Vivienne toward the crosswalk when she suddenly stopped at the red light and grabbed his arm. "Wait. If you weren't planning to stay the night, does that mean you didn't book a room?"

"Was I supposed to?"

Her response was to stare at him, her false lashes making her eyes appear wider and more startled.

His response was to tuck in his chin and draw in a long breath. "I'm guessing you didn't make two reservations?"

"Actually, I didn't make any. Estelle did. She was really determined to get me to Billings and get that contract signed." Vivienne tapped her chin. "But she only emailed me one hotel confirmation. I had assumed she'd emailed yours directly to you."

"Nope. But she'd emailed me every other offer or service I have no use for."

"Maybe she thought you'd be staying with Susie Starlight. But don't worry." Vivienne looked like a woman on a mission as she dashed across the street when the light changed, calling over her shoulder, "I'm sure they'll have extra rooms."

Stepping off the curb to follow her, he had to wait for a group of Harleys making a right turn before catching up to her determined stride right as she crossed into the lobby's entrance. Cole liked being the one to take charge, the one to fix things. But before he could open his mouth to address the clerk behind the registration desk, Vivienne was already speaking.

"Hi, there—" her eyes flickered down to the employee's name tag "—Dave. We have one reservation, but my friend here is also going to need a room."

Friend? That was the second time today she'd called him that and Cole didn't like it any better than the first.

Dave made a whistling sound through his teeth. "We're pretty booked, but I'll see what I can do."

After a few seconds of tapping at his keyboard, Dave shook his head. "Sorry. Even our sister property a few blocks down is sold out. Apparently, there's some sort of wedding convention in town and the Babes on Bikes Rally starts tomorrow, so most of the hotels in the area are at full capacity."

"What do you want to do?" Vivienne, always diplomatic when solving problems, asked Cole. "We might be able to find a single vacancy at a different hotel, but there's not much chance we can get two rooms at the same place."

"It's fine." Cole shrugged to reassure her. "I can sleep in the car."

"Don't be ridiculous," Vivienne replied. "I'm the wedding planner. I should've planned better. If anyone should stay in the car, it should be me."

Before Cole could argue that there was no way he was about to allow her to spend the night crammed into her back seat out in the parking lot, Dave cleared his throat. "If I may point out, the room does have two beds."

"See? You can sleep in the extra bed in my room."

"Are you sure?" Cole whispered to her after Dave passed them each a key card. They'd been doing a great job playing make-believe with each other all day. It shouldn't be a problem for him to keep pretending that he wasn't dying to see her in those Just Married panties she'd gotten in her bride's goody bag.

"Oh, no, we forgot all the swag and totes at the restaurant," she said, making Cole wonder if she could read his mind.

"I'll go get them," he replied, his boot heels already clicking along the marble floor of the lobby as he tore out of the hotel. He needed time to come up with a strategy on how he wasn't going to let his attraction for her make things more awkward. But it took less than thirty seconds to get across the street and the forgotten bags were already waiting for him at the hostess stand.

Not ready to face Vivienne yet, he stopped off at the sundries shop near the hotel elevators. He was going to need a toothbrush and a cold shower if he had any chance of falling asleep so close to her tonight.

But stopping to pick up overnight essentials turned out to be a pointless delay because when he finally knocked on the hotel room door, there was no answer.

## Chapter Ten

Vivienne's speeding thoughts shot into overdrive as she'd ridden in the elevator alone, her pulse hammering with every step she took as she made her way down the empty, carpeted corridor to her room.

Their room.

Steeling herself, she took a deep breath and slid in her key card. As she dragged her suitcase on wheels behind her, the handle caught on the interior doorknob, knocking the do-not-disturb sign to the floor. She quickly scooped it up, a mortified giggle bubbling inside her throat at the thought of how unnecessary that placard would be tonight.

Light spilled out from under the crack of the closed bathroom door and Vivienne tried not to think about what the sound of running water meant. Staring at the two queen-size beds, she scolded herself for overthinking the situation.

The bags containing all their freebies from the day were lined up on the fluffy white coverlet of the first bed, so Vivienne lifted her suitcase and set it on the second one. Looking at the television, she decided that having on a sports or a news channel, even if it was only background noise, would make things feel less intimate. She grabbed the remote control and hit the power button but only got as far as the hotel's main channel displaying a welcome screen and classical music.

When she heard the bathroom door click open, she stood motionless.

"Hey, you're back," Cole said, relief evident in his tone. "I figured if you weren't here when I got out of the shower, I'd have to launch a search party."

"I went to the parking garage to get my suitcase." Her fingers trembled as she fought to stare at the remote control so that she wouldn't look at him. But the smell of lemon soap drifted closer and Cole's nearby voice forced her to raise her eyes.

"Is the TV not working?"

Vivienne's gaze slammed into him and she couldn't blink. He was wearing the same jeans he'd had on today—minus the belt—and not much else. His hair was scarcely towel dried and his bare torso was still damp from his shower.

Desire coiled in her belly and she would've opened another bottle of champagne if she thought it would alleviate her sudden thirst. Vivienne licked her lips, knowing that imbibing in too much sparkling wine was what had gotten her into this situation in the first place. Instructing herself to look anywhere but at the muscular ridges of his chest, she glanced down.

"You have nice feet."

He wiggled his toes in the plush carpet. "What?"

"Your feet. They're nice. I've never noticed them before because I've only seen you in boots."

Several seconds passed before she felt Cole's finger on her chin, lifting her head up to look into his face. "You're going to give me a complex about them if you keep staring."

"Sorry." She straightened her shoulders despite the quivering sensation making its way down her spine, but she didn't pull her head away. Vivienne searched the smoothness of his forehead, the lack of lines implying that he wasn't as confused about their situation as she was. She took in the nearly straight angle of his nose, the tiny bump on the bridge implying he wasn't afraid to fight for what he wanted. She scanned the fullness of his soft lips, the slight parting implying that he was breathing just a little heavier than normal. She landed back on the fringed black lashes of his blue eyes, his dilated pupils implying that he was just as aroused as she was.

His finger grazed along her chin until his palm was cupping her jaw. It could've been the champagne she'd had earlier, or maybe it was the realization that she had the same effect on him that he had on her, but her courage spiked and she suddenly felt the need to make something clear.

"I've never shared a room with a client before."

"Funny thing, I haven't really felt like your client all day." His words were whispery soft, his minty breath a soft caress on her face.

"So then if you aren't my client, I wouldn't be crossing any professional boundaries if I did this."

Even with him in his bare feet, Vivienne still had to rise up onto her tiptoes to kiss him.

The second Vivienne's lips touched Cole's, he exploded. One arm shot around her waist and the other hand dug into the loose hair at the back of her scalp, pulling her in closer. Her body pressed against him, fitting him perfectly. Her mouth slanted over his and he took the invitation to invade. Using his tongue, he sampled and tasted her welcoming warmth.

This was more than kissing. More than weeks of pent-up sexual attraction. More than pretending to be a groom who needed to hire her to plan a fictional wedding. This was real and it was powerful and it was raw.

Vivienne's palms flattened against his chest before sliding up to his shoulders and then down his biceps, as if she was frantically searching for something she'd been missing. Something they'd both been missing. Cole had never felt such an overpowering need for a woman, and the sudden realization of his own defenselessness scared him enough to make him take a step back. Her eyes were slightly dazed, clouded with passion, and her lips were swollen.

Cole was supposed to be the one who always kept a level head. Who always did the right thing. Who always made the safe choices. But if they went any further, he couldn't promise that he wouldn't lose all rational thought and spin completely out of control. Seeing his chest rising and falling under her fingertips, he waited until he could drag in a few ragged breaths before he spoke. "Are you sure?"

Her response was to step back and untie the sash above her hip. Cole had been fantasizing about the feel of the silky, soft fabric of her dresses for the past few weeks and he was almost disappointed that Vivienne was taking it off before he'd had the chance to unwrap it himself.

Almost.

It was like a curtain parting to reveal the hidden view all at once. Watching the entire side of her dress spread open filled him with a raging heat, and all he could do was stand there and let the flames engulf him as she exposed the pink lace of her matching panties and bra. As the material slipped off her shoulders, Cole groaned and reached for her.

Vivienne's mouth matched his, responding with an equal fervor as he walked her back toward the bed. His hands went to her rib cage, sliding behind her until he felt delicate lace underneath his fingers as he unhooked her bra. She moaned as he peeled the fabric forward, cupping her warm, full breasts as they spilled out.

Vivienne's head fell back, allowing him access to her slender neck as he rained kisses down to her collarbone. But the part he wanted to kiss the most was just out of reach. Cole placed his hands on either side of her waist and she squeaked as he lifted her up, standing her on the edge of the bed.

He took a dusky-pink nipple into his mouth and Vivienne's nails dug into his shoulders as she held on to him. He lavished equal attention on the other breast, and when he moved toward the flat plane of her stomach, she gasped.

"Cole," she said, her voice low, coming from the back of her throat, "I still have my shoes on."

He smiled up at her, feeling like the hero he'd always wanted to be when he slid his hand down her thigh, over her knee and lifted her calf. Unstrapping the high-heeled sandals wasn't as easy as he'd anticipated, especially since he got distracted by the sight of the freckle on her upper leg. That was what he'd been waiting for. His tongue flicked out to touch it just as her ankle strap fell from his hands.

Vivienne sighed before hooking her knee around his rib cage and pulling him with her as she lowered them onto the bed. She slipped her hands into his denim waistband, pausing briefly as she fumbled over the button of his fly. It took superhuman strength to push himself off her and rise to his shaky feet.

"I'll be right back," he said as he strode to the bathroom, tugging off his jeans as he returned to the bed. She was lounging against the pillows, her skin looking smoother than the sheets underneath, her panties long gone.

"You came prepared?" She nodded toward the box in his hand.

"I had to buy a toothbrush downstairs and, at the last minute, thought it would be a good idea to have these. Just in case."

"Always thinking about safety and protection," she said before smiling at him. Not wanting to hear any jokes about his nickname, he came down beside her, their bodies eagerly resuming where they'd left off.

Vivienne knew exactly where to touch Cole and how to angle her body to bring him in closer. As their kisses grew more intense, she opened her thighs and his hips settled against her as she rocked up to meet him. She was so warm, so slick with desire, it would have been easy to slide his length inside of her. But he pulled back at the last second to reach for a foil packet on the bedside table.

Cole's fingers quivered as he tore open the package, but instead of taking it from him, her palms covered the backs of his hands as they rolled the condom into place. Together.

When he positioned himself at her entrance again, Vivienne looked up at his face, her eyes wide and trusting, her lips open and delicious. She gave him a nod and that was all it took.

He moved inside of her slowly, carefully balancing his weight on his forearms as he eased them together. But Vivienne's arms locked around his shoulders, her breasts pressing against his chest, and he could no longer hold himself back.

Their speed intensified, their moans matching in frequency until Vivienne shuddered around him and called out his name. A groan tore from his throat as he found his own release.

Vivienne could honestly say that she'd never intended to make love with Cole, but she couldn't say that she hadn't thought about it. It was one thing to have fantasies; it was quite another to be courageous—or reckless—enough to act upon them. Fortunately, her fantasy had exceeded her expectations.

She watched him as he lay on the bed beside her, one arm thrown over his forehead, the other cushioning her neck as he intertwined his fingers with hers. The lights were still on, as was the television with the hotel channel flashing pictures on the screen, and Vivienne chewed on her swollen lip, wondering what people normally did in situations like these.

This was her first one-night stand. Or was it something else? Did Cole intend for there to be more nights than just this one? He'd made his thoughts about marriage abundantly clear when he'd hired her, but did that mean he wasn't a believer in any sort of committed relationship? And was now really the best time to ask him about it?

"I'm going to go take a shower," Vivienne whispered, carefully sitting up so she wouldn't dislodge the tan, sinewy arm covering his eyes. The effects of the champagne were wearing off and the insecurity was setting in. If her dress—or even a towel—had been nearby, she would've dived for it. But she had no idea when she'd last seen either of those things. Cole was sprawled on top of the covers, preventing her from yanking off a sheet and wrapping it around her body. And it would look pretty silly for her to use a pillow to shield her nudity after he'd already seen everything.

Calculating the distance from the bed to the bathroom, she considered making a run for it. But Cole's fingers trailing down her vertebrae to her tailbone made her pause.

"I'll join you," he said, his voice weak. "As soon as the tingling in my body dies down."

She'd made him tingle? Her tummy fluttered and a grin spread across her face, and she suddenly became a lot less self-conscious.

Twelve hours later, though, her confidence slipped again.

On the return trip, while the ride had started out playfully teasing and reliving their thoughts and experiences of the day before, the farther they got from Billings, the quieter the interior of the Jetta became. Vivienne didn't want to read too much into the growing silence, but it was difficult not to. Cole had done all of the driving up until this point and neither one of them had gotten much sleep last night, so maybe that was why there was less talking.

"Why don't we switch and I can drive for a while?" she offered.

"I'm okay," he said, then lost all credibility by covering his mouth for a deep yawn.

"Cole, I phrased it as a question, but it was more of a strong suggestion." When he hesitated in replying, Vivienne continued. "It's okay to let someone take care of *you* once in a while."

He wiggled his eyebrows at her. "I believe those were the same words you used this morning when you were waking me up by using your mouth to—"

"Oh, look." She pointed to the upcoming off-ramp, keeping her face averted so he couldn't see the flush of heat spreading across her cheeks. "A gas station. Let's stop and get some snacks at the convenience store."

Cole chuckled before flicking on the turn signal and pulling off the highway. While he filled the tank, she went inside to use the facilities and splash some cold water on her face. Looking in the mirror, she gave herself a silent pep talk.

*Don't get all embarrassed and awkward now. If he's comfortable enough to tease about your lovemaking sessions, he's clearly not letting things get weird. Just keep things light and pleasant.*

However, keeping her growing nerves at bay was easier said than done. On her way to the cashier, she grabbed some Pringles, then a couple of candy bars. The cheddar-flavored popcorn looked good as well, so she pulled a bag off the shelf. Vivienne scanned the wall of refrigerated cases. It wouldn't be a bad idea to have something to drink, either. Balancing all the snacks in one arm, she pulled open the glass door and reached inside for a Dr Pepper, then chose a bottle of sweet tea for Cole. Maybe the caffeinated beverages would perk them both up.

Thinking about caffeine reminded her of the French toast he'd ordered off the room-service menu this morning and his comment about how he would've been happy to make do with a donut and a coffee. She added a package of powdered donuts to her stack, then went back for the chocolate ones just in case.

By the time she was walking out of the convenience store, she had two plastic bags full of drinks and junk food. Cole had moved the Jetta to a parking spot away from the pump and was standing outside, that smirk of his making her forget all about the pep talk she'd just given herself in the bathroom.

"We could've stopped for a late lunch if you were that hungry." He jutted his chin toward her loaded hands. "There's a burger place right next door."

"Actually, a burger sounds pretty good right about now." What was she saying? Less than four hours ago, she'd plowed through a Denver omelet with hash browns and toast and one of Cole's triangle slices of French toast. There was no possible way she was actually hungry. Which meant she was letting her unfounded worries take hold of her. "But I really need to get back to Lord Nibbles."

"That's right. The infamous Lord Nibbles. How long can a guinea pig go without food and water?"

"He has plenty to eat and I left him with an extra bottle of water. But he's still new and this was my first time away. I'm concerned that he might have undiagnosed separation anxiety."

Cole came around to the front of the car. "Is that what you're concerned about?"

"Mmm-hmm," Vivienne murmured as he leaned in closer.

His lips were only inches from hers. "And here I thought you were regretting things and trying to figure out ways to ditch me once we got back to Kalispell."

Her knees buckled and her tummy turned inside out. She'd thought she'd gotten Cole out of her system last night. And then again this morning. But her body's reaction to his nearness suggested that it wasn't done with him yet. This had the potential to get very complicated if she let it.

"I'd never ditch one of my clients," she said, then planted a very unbusinesslike kiss on his surprised lips. She used the distraction to snatch the keys out of his hand before passing by him and saying, "My turn to drive."

They ended up using the drive-through at the burger place, and Cole dozed off in the passenger seat without finishing his French fries. Vivienne snacked on those and then systematically polished off both packages of donuts, the chips and a soda. By the time they were approaching Flathead Lake, she'd already rehearsed in her mind what she was going to say when they parted.

*It was fun and I enjoyed myself. But we both know where this is headed, so we don't have to pretend otherwise. This week is going to be so busy...*

That last bit still needed work. Vivienne wanted to make it clear that she didn't expect him to call her, and that they could go back to how things had been before they'd spent the night together.

But when they pulled up to her apartment complex and he unfolded himself from her front seat, lifting his arms up over his head to stretch, everything she'd planned to say floated out of her brain. Instead, she offered, "Do you want to come inside?"

## *Chapter Eleven*

"This has been the most challenging wedding rehearsal I've ever had to pull off," Vivienne whispered to Cole as everyone was loading up into their cars to drive from his family's new property into Rust Creek Falls for dinner at the Gold Rush Diner—the first place Zach and Lydia had ever shared a meal together.

The comment took him aback because he'd been watching her direct and orchestrate and explain things for the past hour and she hadn't even broken a sweat. It was like she'd done this a hundred times. In her sleep.

"Really?" Cole asked. "I thought it went pretty smoothly. In fact, too smoothly. But don't worry, I'm ready in case something goes wrong tomorrow."

"There's always something that will go wrong. The

trick is to make the couple and the guests think that everything worked out perfectly."

Was that what she had done to him last weekend? Made him think that he'd experienced the most passionate, carefree night—actually two nights if one counted Sunday, when he didn't leave her house until the wee hours of the morning—in his life, and then politely redirected him at every turn this week when he'd tried to call her.

Vivienne had explained that the final days leading up to the wedding would be chaotic for her and, while she hadn't come right out and said that she didn't want to see him again, Cole got the impression that she was trying to convince him that it was his idea to cool things down between them.

Deep down, he knew that her strategy was for the best. As soon as the wedding was over, he and his brothers would be hitting the ground running, trying to get this land ready for a viable ranching operation. His dad needed him to be focused and not playing an ill-advised game of "chase the wedding planner."

Cole rocked back on his heels. "Are you coming to the rehearsal dinner?"

"Nope." Vivienne shook her head. "I have some last-minute stuff to finish here at the freight house."

"Do you need a hand?" he asked, wanting to cringe at the neediness in his voice.

"I got it," she said, smiling up from her tablet. "You should go and enjoy your family."

He knew he should let her get to work, but he hated

the thought of her staying out here at the property all alone. "How long are you going to be here?"

"Just another hour or two. Why?"

"I don't think you should be here alone after dark."

"Don't worry, Sergeant Save-the-Day." She patted his arm and his lips tightened at her condescending tone. "I'll be fine."

He opened his mouth to tell her about the dangers of being this far away from town, all alone in the Montana wilderness, but one of Lydia's bridesmaids chose that second to walk up.

"Hey, Vivienne, do you have a quick second?" Eva asked. "I know that tomorrow is going to be crazy and I wanted to catch you when you had a second of downtime."

"Of course," Vivienne said brightly, tucking the iPad under her arm.

"I wanted to tell you that I loved the invitations you came up with for Lydia and Zach. How cute was that to make them look like an old-time newspaper? And the way they were addressed? That typeset-style font on the envelopes was absolutely perfect."

"Thanks." Vivienne beamed. "But that wasn't a computer font. I actually found an antique typewriter from the 1920s and did those by hand. My fingertips were numb by the time I finished, but it's those small details that make all the difference. I'm glad you liked them."

"I adored them! Listen, Luke and I are getting married soon and my mom has been bugging me to hire a wedding planner. She's already talked to someone at a company out of Helena called A LaVish Affair, but I kinda thought we should try to go with someone more local."

"Oh, they're fabulous. Having someone local can be convenient, but LaVish works weddings all over Montana."

Eva nodded, but her expression suggested she was slightly confused. "So you think I should hire them?"

"Well, you can't go wrong with Rich LaRue. I know parents can get really emotionally invested when it comes to planning weddings, and even if they have good intentions, they can steer you in directions you may not want to go. My advice would be to meet with Rich and consider whether or not he shares your same vision."

Cole's jaw nearly fell open. Seriously? Vivienne had the prime opportunity to sell herself and land another client and *that* was the advice she chose to give? But before he could stutter out an objection, Eva thanked her and called out, "See you tomorrow."

"Your dad and brother are waiting for you," Vivienne said to him as she discreetly pointed toward Cole's truck.

Garrett leaned over the front seat of the cab and honked the horn, then yelled out the open window, "Let's go, Sarge. The last one there buys the first round."

"My family makes absolutely no sense sometimes," Cole said only loud enough for Vivienne to hear. He pinched the bridge of his nose. "Like, they're all going to go thirsty as they sit there waiting for the last person to show up and pay for their drinks?"

Her chuckle seemed a little forced and she politely said, "Have fun."

It wasn't until he was in his truck that he realized

that Vivienne had never explained why tonight had been such a challenge for her.

With the exception of the awkward rehearsal last night, Vivienne hadn't seen much of Cole in the week leading up to the wedding. But that was by design because she was there to work and not get sidetracked. Her personal life, once again, needed to be placed on the back burner.

Yesterday should have been routine for her. Walk everyone through the ceremony, tell them where to stand and what to do. In fact, the minister was more than capable of doing it for her, but Vivienne had needed to direct her energies toward something that wasn't Cole Dalton.

Yet every time she'd turned around, there he was. Talking to the ring bearer about why he had to slow down and wait for the flower girl, busting out his tool belt when he thought the gazebo needed a few more nails to hold the railing in place, tracking down a wooden picnic bench for his aunt Rita and aunt Mary to sit on, since the rental chairs weren't coming until the following day.

Vivienne found herself constantly focusing on where he was and what he was doing rather than performing her job. If that wasn't bad enough, every time she'd given in to temptation and looked his way, he would tilt the corner of his mouth up and wink at her, completely oblivious to the fact that someone in his family would surely catch them staring at each other.

Then she'd had to make up an excuse about needing

to stay at the freight house to finish up some details. She was afraid that if she joined Lydia's friends and family and the rest of the Dalton clan at dinner, it would only serve to show her what she would be missing once she and Cole resumed their normal lives.

She didn't need Estelle telling her that getting too friendly with her clients was never a good idea. They were paying her to do a job, not to get cozy with the groom's brother. So when she arrived at Sawmill Station at eight o'clock the morning of the wedding, she was relieved nobody else was there.

She had a job to do.

Unlocking the freight house, she walked inside and closed her eyes, envisioning exactly how she wanted the space to look in the next seven hours. It was something she did before the start of every wedding day, like a military general surveying the battlefield before leading his troops to a victory. There were going to be tears and sweat and sacrifices today. But, hopefully, no bloodshed—as long as she remained confident and executed her plans quickly and efficiently.

The rumbling of a diesel truck outside was her call to arms and Vivienne squared her shoulders, marching outside to meet the cavalry. Or rather, the first vendor of the day. She instructed the rental company on how to line the seats for the ceremony, a V-shaped formation with an aisle down the center. Tables were set inside the freight house and, thankfully, Zach and Lydia didn't mind sparing the extra expense of renting double the amount of chairs so that Vivienne wouldn't have to enlist the catering staff or some other unfortunate volunteer to transfer two hundred chairs from the ceremony area outside to the reception inside.

The florist showed up next and stayed to help put out tablecloths and runners. When the caterers got there, Vivienne was able to set them up in the recently remodeled depot so they could use it as a temporary kitchen. Luckily, they'd also brought their own waitstaff, so boxes of dishes and silverware were soon unloaded. After she showed them how she wanted the place settings, she had to remind herself to use the restroom, eat a protein bar and down a bottle of water.

She was using twine to hang mason jars filled with white hydrangeas and sweet peas from long, freestanding iron hooks lining the aisle when Lydia arrived with Jolene, Joanna and Eva. The bride's hands were clasped under her chin and her smile was infectious. "It's looking better than I ever could have imagined!"

"We're not done yet," Vivienne said. "Do you need help carrying stuff inside?"

"That would be great," Lydia replied. "I had a heck of a time getting my dress laid out onto the back seat. I'm afraid it's going to be a wrinkled mess."

Vivienne followed the women to one of their cars, which was loaded down with garment bags and shoe boxes. "Here, take the veil and show your bridesmaids to the bridal suite. I'll get the dress."

"Okay," Jolene snickered as they were walking away, "whose idea was it for us to get ready in an old railcar?"

"That would be Garrett," Cole said, making Vivienne hit her head on the roof of the car as she shot up in surprise. Where'd he come from? They were way too early.

"Where's Zach?" she asked, rubbing the top of her head as she searched the gravel lot for more trucks. "He's not supposed to see Lydia before the wedding."

"He's riding here with Booker and Shawn. I was already set to go and didn't want to wait for them. What can I do to help?"

Vivienne's throat constricted and her palms went damp at the vision of Cole Dalton in his tailored outfit. There'd been a heated discussion regarding the men wearing jeans and matching vests versus tuxedos, but in the end, Vivienne was glad they'd gone with the less formal dove-gray suits. Zach had a penchant for bolo ties, and the cowboy boots were obviously a given. Vivienne had even helped select matching felt Stetsons in a soft shade of granite as groomsmen gifts.

But none of them would look half as good today as Cole did.

She swallowed, then shook her head. "You can't help. I don't want you messing up your fancy duds."

"I don't think carrying some clothes is going to dirty me up," he said, brushing by her to reach inside for the covered gown. "You know, I recently learned that the dress needs to hang outside of the garment bag so it doesn't lose its shape before the bride wears it."

She looked around in alarm. "Did you tell your family about where you attained this newfound knowledge?"

"Nope. And I don't plan to." He winked, cradling the bridal gown in his arms as he walked toward the repurposed railcar.

It was a good thing, too, because if he'd looked at

her a moment longer, he would've seen her suck in her cheeks in frustration. No matter how many blatant winks he risked sending her way, Cole had no intention of telling his relatives that he'd spent the weekend with Vivienne. Which meant that their relationship, for the short forty-eight hours that it had lasted, was a secret.

Thank goodness the world wasn't about to stop and allow her to dwell on it. The hairdresser and makeup artist pulled into the parking area, and from that point forward, Vivienne was in constant motion.

Several more Daltons arrived, and then she had to get Zach into the freight house so that he wouldn't see Lydia. The bartender asked her for a cart to transport bottles of liquor from his truck to the makeshift bar she'd created using the abandoned barrels and some planks of wood. It turned out Uncle Charles had an old wheelbarrow in the back of his truck and Vivienne grabbed some flowers and a hand-lettered sign to incorporate the thing into part of the decorations.

The photographer needed the groom and groomsmen for pictures. The band needed to know where to set up. The minister needed to know who had the marriage certificate.

Buttons broke, missing tea lights were located and last-minute seating arrangements were swapped. Lydia's mother, Rhoda, who was walking her daughter down the aisle to give her away, had forgotten her dress shoes at home and someone had to be dispatched to pick those up.

By the time the first guests began to arrive, Vivienne had already changed from her work clothes into a nondescript dress that would help her blend in with the background. It was her standard operating procedure.

However, every time she saw Cole greet another relative or escort someone to their seat, she was reminded that she would remain in the background. Which had always been okay with her, she thought as she watched Lydia walk down the aisle toward Zach.

Until now.

Cole stuck to his father like glue leading up to the ceremony and immediately afterward, when it was time to pose for all the family photos. That was when Cole, his dad and—he assumed—the rest of his brothers felt his mother's absence the most. No matter how the photographer staged them, there always seemed to be a void where his mother should've been.

While Phil Dalton was happy for his son, as they all were, Cole was probably the only one who noticed how quiet his dad was being. The only one who recognized the lost look in the older man's eyes, as if he wasn't quite sure where to stand or who to talk to next. And when his father didn't look confused, he looked deep in thought, staring off in the distance. There wasn't sadness, exactly, like there had been at his mom's funeral. Yet it didn't feel right to leave his dad on his own so that Cole could take off and celebrate the night away with the other guests.

Vivienne's prior comments about wedding days being fairy tales swirled together with his own painful reminders that love didn't always last. Not everybody got their happily-ever-after.

Sitting at the head table beside his father, he watched Zach and Lydia dance to their first song together. If anyone deserved forever, it was the two of them. Still, that kind of unconditional love wasn't a risk Cole was willing to take for himself.

And just like that, his thoughts of risk had him seeking out Vivienne for the millionth time today. In fact, her whereabouts were never really far from his mind. She hovered near the cake table, speaking with one of the hired servers and arranging the heirloom serving knife set Aunt Mary had insisted they use.

Since Lydia's father hadn't been in her life since she was five years old, Cole's sister-in-law had only one parent there as well, which meant that Mrs. Grant was happy to forgo the traditional father-daughter and mother-son dances. The cutting of the cake was the next item on the agenda. Cole's best man toast would follow, and after that the dancing would commence.

Thirty minutes later, someone clinked a glass and others joined in. The band's lead singer handed Cole a microphone, but his skin felt clammy, his heart felt heavy. It would've been too emotional to say what he was really feeling, so in the end, Cole did what he always did and tried to make light with his toast.

Afterward, he realized that going out of his way to pretend that everything was normal—to pretend that he was *not* the serious, responsible brother—took more out of him than just accepting his mantle of constant dependability. Cole wished he could really be that carefree, that he could just sit back and enjoy the evening, but his nerves remained on edge.

He would've begged Zach to refrain from the traditional garter toss, but Cole knew that begging in the Dalton family signaled a weakness to be mercilessly teased and exploited. And in Rust Creek Falls, home of the infamous wedding punch incident and *The Great Roundup* reality show, determining who was going to get married next was becoming a spectator sport. So when all the single women gathered on the dance floor behind Lydia, Cole knew that was his cue to go outside and get some fresh air.

The June evening was brisk, helping relieve some of the stuffiness of the formal suit Cole had been forced to endure. He was leaning against the east side wall of the freight house, out of sight from the caterers running back and forth between the bigger building and the smaller train depot. Which was why he was surprised to see Vivienne turn the corner.

"Did they send you to round up all the bachelors for the next event?" he asked. Her head tilted in confusion, so he explained. "The garter toss. Are you looking for willing victims?"

"Victims? Oh, I get it. No, actually, that's a tradition I could do without."

"Really? I'd think that'd be a target-rich environment for you to book more clients."

Vivienne let out a deep breath, stretching her arms behind her back. "As you've probably figured out, that's one area of my job that could use some improvement."

"Well, you certainly excel at everything else," he said, unable to look away from the way her stretch caused her breasts to jut forward. She dropped her arms and made a snort. "No, seriously. Don't roll your eyes. This wedding was amazing, and Lydia and Zach are so happy. I even heard a few of my cousins' friends talking about getting some tips from you."

"Trust me, if every job could be like this, this would be the ideal career for me."

"But…?" he prompted.

"But back in business school, nobody told me that the practical side of making money was a lot tougher than the theoretical side. I mean, deep down, I know that in order to be a successful wedding planner, I need to land the big clients, charge the bigger fees and direct them to the biggest vendors so that I can get more referrals, thereby starting the cycle all over again. I just didn't realize I'd have to be a saleswoman to do so. When a bride comes in wanting a simple garden wedding with only twenty guests, Estelle expects me to convince the woman that what she *really* wants is four hundred of her closest friends eating caviar and listening to a twelve-piece orchestra at the luxurious Thunder Canyon Resort."

Her honesty was refreshing. Not that he hadn't already seen the type of woman she was when she'd had plenty of opportunities to look out for her own interests. "Well, I think what you gave Zach and Lydia tonight was better than anything Estelle or Rich LaRue could've done."

His fingertips stroked along her temple, but before he could lean down and kiss her, her phone, which was clipped to the sash of yet another sexy wraparound dress, pinged.

"That's the bartender." Vivienne stood at attention,

as if she was ready to conquer the next battle. "We're running low on ice."

"You stay here and take a breather. I'll go get the ice."

"You're a guest. This is my job."

"Vivienne, you've been going nonstop since when? Ten? Eleven?"

"More like eight," she mumbled.

"See? You need a break. Hide out here and relax for a few more minutes." The music cued up, so Cole knew he was now at least safe from accidentally catching a garter or a bouquet. "Besides, it'll give me an excuse to miss the chicken dance."

He left her with a smile, knowing full well that she wasn't about to stay there lounging about. And he'd been right. By the time he'd delivered the ice and returned to his father's side, Vivienne was helping the waitstaff clear empty glasses and bottles from the abandoned tables. All the people his age were on the dance floor, but Cole didn't feel like kicking up his heels.

He was just ready for this night to be over. He was ready to have Vivienne all to himself again. Cole squeezed his eyelids tightly, squelching the thought that had come out of nowhere. Vivienne wasn't really his, and he knew that. But she had a way of taking his mind off things, and he was simply wishing himself to be anywhere but here.

Everyone finally gathered outside for the big send-off, and when Zach and Lydia pulled away in the rumble seat of the 1930s roadster driven by one of their old friends from Hardin, Cole anxiously turned to his father. "You ready to take off?"

"Truth be told, I'm exhausted. But this is our property now." His father paused, letting the significance of his words sink in. "We're the hosts, so we can't go until everyone else is gone."

"Look, Dad. People are already starting to leave. Booker and Shawn can stay to close up," Cole suggested. "Hell, even Garrett can shut things down, if he ever puts down his beer and gets off that railcar Vivienne set up out back."

"Speaking of Vivienne, I should probably find her and thank her for doing such a good job on everything. She made it real fancy, but it also felt simple and down-home. Not too showy. I only wish your—" Phil's voice cracked, then he sniffed and carried on. "It's too bad your mama couldn't have been here to see how perfectly it all came together. She always did love a wedding."

As his father turned to head back toward the freight house, Cole's boots remained rooted to the grass near the gravel parking area. The guilt he'd been holding back all evening raced through him, and he looked up to the darkening sky, which was still streaked in a haze of orange and pink from the late-setting sun. His fist clenched as he crossed his arms in front of his chest, and his throat clogged when he whispered, "Sorry you couldn't be here, Mama. Sorry for letting you down."

## Chapter Twelve

"I'm gonna catch a ride back to the ranch with your aunt and uncle," Cole's father told him when he finally made his way back to the freight house. They were coming outside as Cole was walking inside, Uncle Charles yawning and Aunt Rita carrying one of the centerpieces. Most of the guests were already gone and the tables had been cleared of dishes. "I couldn't find that pretty wedding planner, but I know she's still hopping around here somewhere. That gal's got energy to spare and she's too quick for me."

Cole waved off his old man. "Get on home, Dad. I'll find Vivienne and thank her for us."

"You do that." His dad squeezed his shoulder. Was it his imagination, or was there a little twinkle in Phil Dalton's tired eyes?

Cole was a cowboy, a former Marine. He was used to being on his feet all day. But his dressy ostrich boots were still relatively new and had been pinching him all night. Still, that didn't stop him from helping the band haul their equipment outside or carrying the last load of stainless-steel trays to the caterer's van.

"Cole, you don't have to help," Vivienne said as she folded the last tablecloth. "I told you I'd lock up when everyone left."

"I know." He shrugged, not having the emotional energy to argue. Instead, he asked, "What are we doing with all the tables and chairs?"

"The rental people are coming tomorrow morning to get those, so just leave them where they are."

By the time he clicked the padlock into place on the sliding doors of the freight house, the only two cars remaining in the gravel lot were his truck and Vivienne's Jetta. She was standing on the platform in front of the train depot, a cardboard box in one arm and her trusty tote bag hooked on the other.

He met her at the steps. "These country roads get pretty dark at night. Why don't I drive you back to Kalispell?"

"Cole, I'd tell you that I'm more than capable of driving on a two-lane highway and there's no need for you to go out of your way like that, but then you'd insist. I'd say that I don't want to leave my car here for someone to see and then you'd counter that you could leave your truck here instead. To be honest, I'm way too exhausted to go through all that arguing."

"Good, give me your keys."

"Then how will you get back?"

He looked over at his truck. Did it really matter how he got back? He was well aware that driving Vivienne home was just an excuse to spend more time together. But, like her, he was too tired to rationalize it. He just wanted to be with her. "I'll follow you, then. Make sure you get home safely."

The drive took almost thirty minutes and all that time alone in the dark cab of his truck gave him too much time to think. To feel. To let his emotions get the better of him. So when he met her in the parking lot of her apartment complex, he was filled with a raging need and a determination that he'd never experienced before. She hadn't even gotten her purse out of the back seat when he spun her to him, pressed her back against her car and planted his lips on hers.

With all the emotion throbbing through him today, the kiss consumed him, filling him with more passion than anything he'd ever experienced. Nothing mattered but sinking into her embrace, into her depths. He didn't care about anything but the fact that her mouth was welcoming him eagerly and that she was clinging to him with equal desperation.

If someone had asked him what was going through his mind, he couldn't even put into words what this sensation was and he definitely wasn't ready to describe it, let alone think it. All he knew was that being with Vivienne at this exact second felt right. It felt perfect.

Vivienne had been well aware that Cole was just doing his hero thing, offering to follow her home. Yet something about the way they'd come together last night had been different, more intense than it had been when they'd first made love. As she stretched out on her bed beside him the following morning, she was careful to not wake him up. She was also careful to not let her thoughts stray too far. After attending a successful wedding, it was easy for people to slip into the kind of romantic afterglow that made them think their hearts were ready to conquer the world.

Not that Cole had been waxing poetic. In fact, she'd noticed how stoic he'd been throughout the ceremony and how he'd purposely avoided most of the customary wedding festivities. And neither one of them had been doing much talking after he kissed her in the parking lot, so it should've been easy to replay in her mind his previous jokes about matrimony.

The problem was, as much as she'd given up on marriage lately, Vivienne hadn't given up on falling in love. Maybe it was just the aftereffects of witnessing such a beautifully poignant ceremony and successful reception last night, but she had a pretty good idea that what she was currently feeling for Cole would cause the self-professed eternal bachelor to run for the hills.

She blew out her breath in frustration, dislodging a loose curl on her forehead. How could she have let herself get so caught up? She was smarter than this.

Cole groaned beside her, keeping his eyes shut as he flexed his arm and pulled her closer. His warm body surrounded her and erased every rational argument she'd just outlined in her head.

Lord Nibbles's exercise wheel squeaked to life from

the living room, where Vivienne had moved his cage after the first night she had him and realized that he was a nocturnal animal. She looked at the watch she'd been in too much of a hurry to take off last night.

Hmm—6:08 a.m. It was unusual for him to be up at this time. It was also unusual for him to use the noisy exercise wheel. He'd done the same thing last week when she'd left him overnight to go to Billings.

Did guinea pigs hold grudges?

She slipped out of bed and padded across the cheap, thin carpet of her apartment to give him some attention. But the prim and proper chap ignored her finger extending into the unhinged door, his little wiggly nose lifted into the air. Vivienne went to the cupboard and pulled out a Nutter Butter cookie. There was no way he'd ignore that.

"Are you supposed to be feeding him peanut butter?" Cole asked from the doorway. He was wearing nothing but a pair of boxer briefs, riding low on his hips, and Vivienne's heart spun like the exercise wheel inside the cage.

"It might be a little fattening, but Lord Nibbles isn't watching his waistline."

Cole's eyes darted down to the hem of Vivienne's tank top. "Speaking of waistlines, I enjoyed watching yours last night when you were straddling—"

"Can I make you some eggs?" she interrupted, making an about-face toward the minuscule kitchen and popping a cookie into her own mouth. She continued between bites, slurring her words, "Maybe shum coffee?"

Cole's chuckle was low and deep. "So what does a

wedding planner do after the wedding? Are you now off duty until the next one?"

She'd barely swallowed before shoving another cookie in, reminding herself of Estelle, who would use the dying end of a cigarette to light a fresh one. "What nexsht one?"

"Well, you're still planning mine, right?"

Vivienne turned around to switch on her coffeemaker. Not necessarily because she needed the caffeine, but because she didn't want to face him for this conversation. "I, uh, figured that now that Zach's wedding is over and I'm not at risk of getting fired beforehand, you and Susie Starlight would be calling yours off this week."

"Hmm," he said, coming up behind her, sliding his warm hands over her hips. He whispered against her hairline behind her ear, "I wouldn't mind having a few more consultations with my planner."

*Consultations.* Her brain tried to concentrate on that one word, but it was quickly overridden by the tightening of her thighs and the ticklish pricking of the stubble from his jaw rubbing against her neck.

"I thought you had a family ranch you needed to get running."

Cole sighed as he straightened up, leaving a cool breeze along her shoulder where his warm breath had just been. "You're right. We're putting up fence all this week. And my dad has an architect coming tomorrow to show him the blueprints for the new house and barn. Hey, is that my binder?"

Vivienne looked across the open kitchen to the white

plastic binder on her coffee table. Besides forging Susie's signature on the contract, she hadn't touched it since they'd returned from Billings.

She was saved from answering as he walked the few steps to retrieve it. "It looks way thinner than the one you had for Zach and Lydia."

Grabbing another cookie, Vivienne followed him to the living room. "That's because most couples—you know, the ones who actually have real plans to get married—tend to provide me with lots of ideas to fill up the pages."

"Well, I'm fresh out of ideas." He spread his hands out wide. "Besides, you outdid yourself yesterday. There's no way I could come up with something better than that."

His tone was playful, but something nagged at Vivienne.

"Really? Because I got the impression that you weren't really enjoying yourself last night."

Tension flickered across his face before he shrugged. "It wasn't that. It's just none of that stuff is my thing, you know?"

What could she do but nod? Cole had made himself abundantly clear in that regard. At the same time, he'd also made it pretty clear that he wasn't planning on stopping whatever this was that they had between them. It wasn't that Vivienne was opposed to having a casual relationship, as long as both of them knew that things weren't headed in a different direction. One thing she'd learned from her parents' marriage was that she didn't want to go back and forth. She didn't want this emotional tug-of-war raging inside of her.

As she was the kind of person who thrived on organization and communication, compulsion forced her to lay it all out on the table.

"Look, Cole. I think we both have a lot of things going on in our lives right now. You've got the ranch and Lord knows I need to focus on my career, or else I'm not going to have one. Which means Lord Nibbles and I can kiss this glamorous apartment—" she gestured toward the nondescript rental furniture "—goodbye. Anyway, neither one of us probably has time for anything more than some casual fun. Do you agree?"

Initially, when she'd started talking, his face had been like stone, hard and unreadable. His eyes had been steady but not panicked. That was a good thing, right? Twisting her bottom lip between her teeth, she waited for his response. And tried not to stare at the muscular ridges of his abdomen, because if she glanced down, she would surely lose her nerve to continue this conversation and wind up pushing him back onto the beige tweed sofa to have her way with him.

After several seconds of uncomfortable silence, his face finally relaxed and his smirk suggested that he was relieved that she wasn't asking him for any sort of commitment. "I'm definitely a fan of the fun part—"

His phone let out a shrill ring from the bedroom, and he cut off whatever else he'd been about to say as he strode to the bedside table.

"What's wrong, Garrett?" he said by way of answer. Vivienne couldn't hear the other side of the conversation, but Cole was quick to reply. "Because you never call me after a night of drinking unless there's something wrong."

He ran a hand through his short, dark hair, then balanced the cell phone between his ear and his shoulder as he pulled on his gray slacks from the night before. "Uh-huh," he said, then paused a few more beats. "You've got to be kidding me!"

Filled with a sudden sense of worry, Vivienne walked to the side of the bed so she could be there to lend whatever support Cole needed.

"Fine. Text me the address and I'll come pick you up." He yanked on the white button-down shirt she'd practically torn off him last night, then made a grunting sound. "And you guys all told me the Share My Location app was overkill. I'll meet you outside in a minute."

Cole disconnected the call and tossed the phone onto the bed as he tugged on his boots.

"What happened?" Vivienne asked.

"Well, speaking of fun and casual," he said, not looking up, "Garrett had a bit too much to drink last night and went home with one of the waitresses from the catering company. Unfortunately, he woke up in the waitress's roommate's bed instead and isn't sure how that happened. He snuck out a few minutes ago and is outside in the parking lot."

"Here? In *my* parking lot?"

"Yep. He was going to call Shawn to come pick him up, but I installed this app on their phones so that— Never mind. Anyway, he got an alert that my phone was only a few blocks away and, wanting to get out of

Dodge before the waitress or her roommate woke up, he did the walk of shame over here."

Cole put his phone and wallet in his pocket, grabbed his keys and was almost to the bedroom doorway before he turned around and pulled Vivienne into his arms. "Sorry my brother is a dumbass. I'll call you later."

His parting kiss was short but thorough and left little doubt that he would in fact be calling her soon. He scooped something off the coffee table on his way out the door. Sergeant Save-the-Day was off on his next mission.

It wasn't until she lowered her fingers from her swollen lips that she realized he'd taken the white binder with him.

It was later that night before Cole allowed himself to text Vivienne.

She couldn't have been clearer that she wanted to keep their relationship as status quo, which was fine with him. Especially since he'd expected her to call things off altogether. When she'd begun her speech about them both having busy lives, he'd had to work to keep his face from showing any disappointment, because even though he didn't want anything serious, he also wasn't quite ready to stop seeing her.

That was why he kept his message simple. Drove by Sawmill Station. The rental company picked up the tables and chairs. Thought you might want to know.

Sitting in his cousin's former bedroom, he stared at the pink ruffle along the edge of the curtain as he waited for what felt like an hour but was probably only a couple of minutes. Finally his phone vibrated in his hand with her reply. Thanks. How's your brother?

He let out a breath. They were still good.

Stupid and hungover, Cole typed, then debated whether or not he should text her *Talk to you soon* or *Can't wait to see you again*. But he didn't want to sound too needy. He ended up going with a simple Good night.

The week after the wedding was busier than the week leading up to it. It was time for the real work on the ranch to begin, and Cole was up before dawn and dragging his tired body home well after dark every night. He tried to find reasons to text Vivienne, but most of them were asinine questions about the wedding emails Estelle had him subscribed to. What he really wanted to ask was if he could see her this weekend. He remembered that she was working on a big sixtieth birthday party for some wealthy Kalispell socialite, but he couldn't remember the exact date.

On Thursday, he was on an all-terrain vehicle they'd borrowed from Uncle Charles, digging holes for fence posts, when his cell phone vibrated on his hip. So far, the ground had been hard and the midday sun had been unforgiving, but seeing Vivienne's name on his screen made him grin.

"Hello?" he said, putting the phone to his ear.

"Uh, hi, Cole. It's Vivienne Shuster over at Estelle's Events." Her tone was hesitant yet professional, and there was only one reason she'd feel the need to give her last name and place of employment to the guy she'd slept with just a few days ago. Estelle was listening.

"Miss Shuster," he replied, suddenly annoyed by

their formal pretense. At one time, it had seemed amusing and slightly wicked to trick her boss. Now Cole wished everything was out in the open, that they didn't need a reason to call each other or to see each other. "I almost didn't recognize your voice."

There was a brief pause and Cole mentally kicked himself for the sarcastic comment. But then Vivienne continued. "The reason I'm calling is that Estelle would like me to come get the planning binder from you."

"The what?"

"The planning binder. You know, the one you took last weekend when your *fiancée* was in town for your brother's wedding? You guys were going to try to fill out some more of it, maybe add some pictures of ideas you wanted to incorporate for your own big day?" Her emphasis implied that she was hoping he'd go along with whatever excuse she'd told her boss, but it took him a second to realize why she was asking about the binder.

That's right, he'd taken the thing from her apartment on Sunday. At the time, it had been a split-second decision, almost a subconscious last resort to ensure that he still had a reason to talk to her despite all her hemming and hawing about the status of their relationship. "How soon do you need it?"

"No rush," she started, then there was a muffled sound as if she'd covered the mouthpiece of her phone. "Actually, if I could pick it up tomorrow, that'd be great."

"Tomorrow works," he said eagerly, before realizing that his dad and the three of his brothers who weren't on their honeymoon would be out here working with him. He didn't want them asking why he needed to meet with Zach's wedding planner. Cole was about to suggest meeting her in Rust Creek Falls, but then someone in town might ask the same question. Instead, he said, "Actually, I have to come to Kalispell to pick up some supplies for the corrals we're going to start next week. Why don't I meet you at Matilda's for lunch and I can give it to you then?"

His gut twisted while he waited for her reply. He'd been hoping to ask her out on a proper date, but suggesting a business lunch was the best he could come up with while still maintaining the charade for her boss.

"That would be great," she said, and Cole's stomach unclenched at the relief in her voice. "I have a new client coming in at one, so I'll need to be back to the office in time for that."

"I'll pick you up at eleven thirty, then."

"No need for that. I can meet you there. See you tomorrow." Vivienne disconnected first and Cole stared at her name vanishing from his screen.

Putting away his phone and picking up his shovel, he tried not to dwell on her rushed response or her refusal of his offer for a ride to the restaurant. All that mattered was that he would be seeing her tomorrow. He turned the volume up on his iPod and tried to figure out where he could find some pictures to shove into his pretend-wedding-planning binder.

## Chapter Thirteen

"I'm so sorry I'm late," Vivienne told Cole, who slid out from the booth and stood up when she arrived for lunch. "Estelle wanted to reschedule her weekly hair appointment so that she could come with us and I had to convince her that I could handle it."

"No problem." His good manners didn't surprise her, but she was definitely taken aback by his kiss hello. She'd turned her face just in time to present him with her cheek instead, praying that nobody else in the diner had noticed. Kalispell wasn't as small a town as Rust Creek Falls, but people here still talked.

Especially Matilda, the owner, who had no problem asking her customers personal questions.

The woman appeared with an iced tea for Cole and a Dr Pepper for Vivienne, her plastic cat's-eye glasses not hiding her raised eyebrows. "So, Viv, I heard from this handsome stud that you did a great job on his brother's wedding out in Rust Creek."

Vivienne's tight smile remained firmly in place despite the heat rising all the way up to her hairline. She nodded, then put the straw to her mouth for a long, slow sip to avoid further conversation. Thankfully, the lunch rush hour was beginning, and Matilda had other customers to chat with.

"I hope you don't mind," Cole said, nodding toward her red plastic cup of soda. "I knew what you would want to drink, but I wasn't sure how stressed you'd be today, so I haven't ordered lunch yet."

Amazed, Vivienne sat back in the booth. Had anybody ever ordered for her before? At least correctly? Growing up, her mother had always monitored Vivienne's intake of food, suggesting lighter portions and insisting that boys didn't like girls who ate more than them. And Estelle, on the rare occasions she'd taken pity on Vivienne for having to work through breaks, would simply pick up two of whatever she was having. Vivienne was usually the one seeing to everyone else's preferences. Nobody had ever really paid attention to hers. "Thanks."

"I've been meaning to ask you," Cole said as he watched her slurp down half of her Dr Pepper. "What exactly does Estelle do? Because she wasn't at the wedding last Saturday and she didn't attend the bridal expo. As far as I can see, you do all the labor."

"She used to be much more active, back in the day. But times have changed and Estelle is of the opinion that if something ain't broke, don't fix it. When she hired me, I was fine with the distribution of duties because it let me do the part I loved and she took care of all the behind-the-scenes things, like drawing up contracts and paying the bills. But now that she's slowing down and becoming more pushy and cranky with the clients, we're not getting as much business as we used to. But the birthday party we're doing this weekend is for one of her friends, so she'll be more hands-on with that."

A different waitress approached and Vivienne ordered the Cobb salad, then changed her mind and got the chicken potpie lunch special, which came with a side salad. There was always too much gravy in Matilda's potpies, so she requested a side of mashed potatoes to help soak some up. "And I better order the blackberry cobbler now, since I have to leave in forty-five minutes."

"I'll do the Western bacon burger with onion rings, please," Cole said, handing the waitress their menus. He looked at Vivienne, one brow raised. "I hope it's your one-o'clock clients that are stressing you out, not me."

She forced a chuckle, but it was definitely not Dolores Stack's anniversary party next week that had Vivienne wanting to eat like a starved grizzly bear getting ready for hibernation. Dr. and Mrs. Stack had the same party at the same country club every single year and Vivienne could throw it blindfolded. But she didn't tell Cole that. Instead, she changed the subject. "So how's the ranch coming along?"

"Good. My dad and I met with the architect who is designing the new buildings. Now we need to figure out who is going to live where."

"What do you mean?" She finished off the rest of her soda and wished the diner served appetizers or something other than the basket of prepackaged crackers.

"Well, my dad will live in the main house, obviously, but he wants each of us to build our own place on the property, which is generous of him, but I don't like the idea of him being alone. Booker, Shawn and Garrett—especially Garrett—are all single, and while I don't see anything changing on that front anytime soon, they're already chomping at the bit to have their own space. Zach's the only one of us who would have any foreseeable need for a house, but he's going to be living in town with Lydia for a while. That leaves me to stay with my Dad and keep an eye on things."

Vivienne's heart swelled at his love for his father. Of course he planned to live with his dad. Cole was the family caretaker. But it was also further proof that he had no intention of ever having his own home, his own family. This was why she hadn't seen the man all week and she'd purposely tried to keep the limited messages between them casual. There was no long-term for them.

"So tell me about the design for the main house," Vivienne said. The topic of plan layouts and decorating were familiar enough that she could easily follow along, yet neutral enough that she wouldn't have to discuss her own future and lack of picket-fence expectations.

Cautioning herself not to shovel her food into her mouth so quickly, Vivienne listened to Cole talk about the layout, the number of bedrooms and a ridiculously large stone fireplace using some of the creek-bed rocks they'd salvaged after the fire at their ranch, Dalton's Gulch.

It was the perfect opportunity to ask him about his past. "Do you miss your old ranch?"

He paused, an onion ring halfway to his mouth. "Sometimes. It's weird. When I shipped off to boot camp, I was eighteen years old, a fresh-faced baby who wanted nothing more than to serve others and save lives. But I was so homesick, like physically sick to my stomach. At night, I was too exhausted to feel anything, but I used to lie in my bunk every morning, willing myself not to puke. We could send letters and that helped, but we didn't have access to phones or anything. Thirteen weeks later, my mom and dad came to my graduation at the recruit depot in San Diego, and it was like a miracle cure. It made me realize I wasn't missing my home, I was just missing my family. After that, it didn't matter where they stationed me. As long as I could talk to my parents every so often, I was fine. So I guess that's the long way of saying I don't really miss Dalton's Gulch, because my dad and brothers aren't there anymore. But I'll always miss my mom."

Vivienne reached across the table, laying her hand on his. "I'm so sorry, Cole."

She'd been around him enough to know that he liked fixing things, pretending that he was above being bothered by his own problems. So when she saw that his eyes were slightly glassy, as though a mist was covering them, she wasn't surprised that he immediately shrugged off her sympathy and looked up at the ceiling before giving her a little smirk. "It is what it is."

The man was too stubborn to succumb to something as human as tears. In fact, he'd flipped his hand over and was now using his fingers to stroke the inside of her wrist as he tried to change the subject. "What about your parents? Has your dad moved back home yet?"

"Ugh." Vivienne picked up a spoon and began digging into the vanilla ice cream melting over her cobbler. "He came home, but now my mom has moved into the apartment. She says it's *her* turn to live the bachelorette lifestyle this time."

"I can't believe they keep an apartment just for when they have fights."

"Technically, it's my apartment. Or it was. I was living there when they had one of their longer breaks. Unlike you, home is wherever my parents are *not*. So I sublet the unit to my dad and found the place where I'm living now. The rent is a bit more than I can afford, but I try to tell myself that I can't put a price on peace of mind, you know?"

Vivienne immediately regretted her words when the bill came and Cole's tanned, muscular forearm shot out to grab it.

"I'm not broke," she argued. Technically, it wasn't a lie because she wouldn't necessarily be broke unless she lost her job. "You don't always have to pay for me."

"I know." Cole gave her an indulgent smile, which made Vivienne feel even more like a charity case, as he stood up to retrieve his wallet, peeling two twenty-dollar bills out and throwing them on the bill. "I better get you back for your next client."

Annoyance at his constant attempts to take care of her was prickling at her.

"I can get back on my own," Vivienne said, a bit too

defensively. Then she amended, "You wouldn't want to risk having Estelle see you. We've had two calls this week from potential clients in Rust Creek Falls raving about the freight house, and she wants to talk to you about converting the place into a proper venue for more weddings."

"Lord save me from any more weddings or wedding talk," Cole replied, placing a hand on her back as they walked toward the exit. "Which reminds me. I need to grab that binder thingy out of my truck for you."

It turned out his truck was parallel parked a block away from the diner, which meant that they were only another block away from her office. Surely, he wouldn't insist on walking her the rest of the way. As much as she wanted to soak up every minute they had together, it was a bad idea to get too attached.

Cole used his key to unlock the passenger door. Looking back on it, Vivienne wished she would've stayed on the sidewalk near the tall cab of his truck instead of waiting for him by the back bumper. That way, when he pulled her into his arms for a long and thorough kiss goodbye, Estelle wouldn't have seen them as she was driving down the street.

"I trusted you" was the first thing out of Estelle's mouth when Vivienne walked up to the office. Actually, the first thing out of her mouth was the cigarette she'd just lit. But the nicotine apparently wasn't having a calming effect.

Her boss was standing outside the front door, her petite frame blocking the entrance, forcing the confrontation to happen where anyone could walk by and overhear them. "I trusted you with my clients, with my reputation, with my entire business, yet this is how you repay me? You start up an affair with one of our grooms?"

"It's not an affair." Vivienne was quick to defend herself before she clamped her jaw shut at the risk of further implicating herself. But it really wasn't an affair. At least, not the kind Estelle meant. Vivienne clung to the binder Cole had given her before he'd driven off, thankfully oblivious that Estelle had just busted them.

"You were kissing him in full daylight out on the street!" It appeared that steam was coming from Estelle's ears, but it could also have been smoke from the heavy cigarette puffing she was doing between sentences. "I bet Susie Starbright would beg to differ."

It was Starlight, and she was a horse. But it wasn't like Vivienne could tell her boss that. Or justify her behavior in any way. If she explained that there was no bride to begin with, no wedding to plan, then she'd be admitting that she'd lied to Estelle from the get-go. That she'd had Cole sign a contract and pay them a deposit under false pretenses. The liability for that would be far worse than having her boss think she would break up a marriage. As much as Vivienne hated having her character called into question, it was better to be thought a home wrecker than a disreputable fraud.

"I knew you were too good to be true," Estelle muttered, causing Vivienne to wonder what all that "I took a chance on you" attitude Estelle had projected less than a month ago had been about.

"Perhaps we should talk about this later," Vivienne

suggested calmly. "I have a new client coming in at one, remember?"

"Oh, no, you don't." Estelle pointed her finger, the long ash barely hanging on to the tip of her cigarette. "*I* have a client coming at one. You have some want ads in the paper you need to start looking through for your next job."

Want ads? The woman was so old-fashioned she didn't even know that people nowadays found jobs online. Wait. Panic washed through her. "Are…are you firing me?"

"You can't think I'd allow you to stay on my payroll and sleep with the next groom that walks in the door?"

The allegation was worse than a slap in the face. Not only was she accusing Vivienne of being a slut, she was accusing her of being a predatory one at that. Vivienne was frozen in place. How could she make Estelle understand?

"But I brought in more clients…" Okay, so Cole wasn't a legitimate client, but he was a paying one. And the one coming this afternoon was another Rust Creek Falls bride who'd called her after Lydia and Zach's wedding.

The big shoulder pads in Estelle's 1980s style suit jacket lifted in odd angles as she extended her arms across the front door of the office. "If you think I'm letting you step one foot inside my business, you better think again. There's no way I'm giving you another second of access to my clients and my vendors and all the contacts I've spent decades building."

Vivienne's mouth hung open in shock as her heart squeezed together on the inside. She'd put plenty of hours and sweat into building up this business as well, and now Estelle wasn't even going to let her collect her personal things?

"My laptop is in there," she said, her voice weak and pathetic. "My phone charger and…" Vivienne couldn't think of what else belonged to her.

A retired couple walked toward the entrance of the CPA's office next door and it became evident that standing out here and pleading with Estelle was causing even more of a scene. Thankfully, Estelle lowered her raspy voice and said, "I'll send a messenger with your final paycheck and all the things you left behind, including that stash of peanut butter pretzels and granola bars you keep in the credenza. If you leave quietly, I won't tell everyone we do business with that you broke up a marriage."

Vivienne flinched. It was one thing to be fired because her boss of over three years thought so poorly of her. It was another thing to become a pariah of the event-planning industry. If a rumor like that got out, she'd never get another job.

Her mouth opened and closed several more times, but the disgust coming out of Estelle's eyes was too intense, too hate filled. Vivienne had always prided herself on her diplomacy skills, on being the voice of reason in the most emotionally charged situations. Yet there was nothing she could say to save herself.

She couldn't even hold her head up as she turned and walked away, still clutching Cole's binder to her chest.

## Chapter Fourteen

Four days later, Cole was looking down at his phone, wondering why Vivienne hadn't responded to any of his texts since their lunch on Friday. He'd known she was busy with an event over the weekend, but it wasn't like her to not respond at all. Unless she was trying to cool things down between them.

His palms itched and his mind immediately went to the worst-case scenario, the way it always did when he started worrying about a loved one.

The thought stopped him cold. A loved one? He didn't actually love Vivienne, did he? Because if he fell for her, that would put him at risk of losing her and getting hurt.

No, he told himself. He didn't love her. This feeling was nothing more than a powerful sense of responsibility. He'd experienced this with countless people. Squad mates, his cousins' friends, hell, even horses. As though to prove it to himself, Cole slipped his phone into his holder and went back to work on the never-ending fence line.

Even with the train depot and freight house, the acreage on this property was almost twice the size of their last ranch. And they were starting from scratch. He could've stayed back with his brothers, working on the new barn and stables. But he'd been in a bad mood since Monday, when he'd tried to call Vivienne and it had gone to voice mail. Garrett had asked if it was a woman who had him so twisted up and Cole reminded his brother that after the mess he'd gotten himself into the night of the wedding, he shouldn't be talking to anyone about problems with women.

The sound of the diesel engine of his dad's Dodge forced him to shove away all thoughts of Vivienne. Cole walked over to the dirt path where his father had parked and was now exiting the crew cab.

"You didn't come to the barn for lunch," Phil said, holding up a small blue cooler by the handle.

See, this was what his family did. They looked out for each other. Cole wasn't the only Dalton who had a tendency to be overprotective. "Thanks, Dad."

"You know, you *are* allowed to take a break occasionally," his old man said.

Cole responded with a slight shake of his head. There was too much to do and too much to think about. He took the insulated jug off the back of his all-terrain vehicle and used the spout to grab a quick drink before letting the cool water spray onto his face and then his forearms. Pulling a handkerchief out of his jeans pocket, he dried his hands before wiping off the back of his neck.

"Son," his father said, putting a leathery tan hand on Cole's shoulder. "I know you think you're the only one who can get this ranch up and running. But you're not going to be any use to the rest of us if you're out here until all hours dragging yourself till you're in the ground."

"I know my limitations."

"Do you?"

Cole didn't answer, because it was a well-disputed opinion in his family that he had a tendency to work himself ragged trying to do everything for everybody. His brothers called it a hero complex, but Cole called it serving a need.

"How's that pretty little wedding planner doing?"

"What?" Cole's damp head whipped around at his father's sudden change of direction.

"Vivienne. You know, the gal you had lunch with last week?"

Cole squinted. "How did you know I had lunch with her?"

"You think you're the only one who likes to keep tabs on where his family is?"

"Hmm. At least it's good to know everyone's finally using the locator app I installed on your smartphones."

"Pfshh." Phil waved him off. "Don't need that technology nonsense when I've got good old-fashioned small-town word of mouth."

"Since when did you become a gossipy old man?"

"There's a difference between speaking gossip and listening to it," his dad said, and Cole lifted a brow. "And I'm not about to reveal my sources, but some of the same people who shop at the hardware supply in Rust Creek Falls also occasionally go into Kalispell to get their pie fix. I mean, Eva-Rose's pies are mighty fine, but Matilda has a heavy hand with the whipped cream, you know. Ever since this person's wife got on him about his cholesterol, he's had to steer clear of Daisy's Donut Shop and sneak out of town whenever he wants a proper dessert."

"You'd think the mailman would be more careful talking about who he ran into in Kalispell if he didn't want his wife to find out."

Phil's eyes widened in surprise at Cole's accurate guess that Barney was his so-called source, but he quickly recovered. "Anyway, my point is that you've been spending a lot of time with Vivienne Shuster, and the way I heard it, the two of you were looking pretty cozy out on the sidewalk when you kissed her goodbye."

Cole's mouth tilted at the memory of that kiss. It had packed quite a punch, and at the time neither one of them had seemed to care who might see them. But now that Vivienne hadn't talked to Cole in a few days, maybe he'd misinterpreted things.

"So, you are dating her?" His dad must've noticed the mix of expressions that crossed Cole's face every time he thought of Vivienne.

"I guess you could say we were dating. But I don't exactly know what's going on between us right this second." Cole wasn't one to talk about his relationships with anyone, especially his family. But his father didn't appear to be in a hurry to take off anytime soon. In fact, the older man scooted his hip onto the supply bed of the ATV. Cole sighed. "I haven't heard from her in a few days."

"I bet that must be killing you." Phil Dalton didn't tease his boys often, but when he did, the resemblance between him and Garrett was uncanny. They had the same devilish grin. In fact, their mother used to say that all her sons had that playful smirk.

"Why do you say that?"

"Because God forbid someone doesn't ever return your call." As soon as the words were out of his dad's mouth, pain flashed in the older man's eyes and he sucked in his whiskered cheek before blowing out a breath. "I'm sorry, Cole. I didn't mean to bring that up. You're right to worry about that sort of thing. We all are."

Cole's lungs felt hollow, and he folded his arms across his chest as though he could keep his heart from sinking any further.

"I know you guys all make fun of me for being uptight about phones, but I was the one who..." Cole couldn't bear to finish the last sentence.

"Do you think you're the only one who feels guilty for what happened to your mom? Hell, son, she was *my* wife and I wasn't able to protect her any more than you were."

None of the men liked talking about the circumstances surrounding Diana Dalton's death. However, while he was sure that all his brothers held on to a sense of guilt at not being able to save her, Cole was ultimately the one responsible.

When it happened, he'd just returned stateside after a deployment to Iraq, waiting for his commanding officer to approve his leave paperwork so he could hop a plane to Montana. At the same time, his father and brothers were hauling feed to a herd of cattle at the far end of their property when a fast-moving wildfire headed directly toward their ranch house. His mom had been home and probably didn't even see or smell the fire until it was too late. Her husband and sons had tried to call her from their cell phones, but the landline wires had already gone down in the blaze and she didn't answer her own cell—which was later found in the back of her burned car.

"Cole, saving people is what you do. I get that. You've always been in the right place at the right time, but this was one instance when you weren't. Even if you hadn't been thousands of miles away, you couldn't have saved her."

"No, but I could have prevented it."

"You think you could've prevented a massive wildfire that scorched tens of thousands of acres in under an hour?"

"No, Dad. But I was the last one she spoke to on her cell phone. Right before she set it down inside her trunk so she could carry in all the groceries." Cole's throat tightened as he pushed out the words. "The groceries she'd just gone to the store to get to cook my favorite homecoming meal for me."

It was hard to meet his father's eyes, but his dad's stare was too long and intense to escape. The older man spread his arms. "Get over here, son."

But Cole's feet felt heavy in his boots and he didn't take a step. After his mother's devastating death, he'd been the one to pull his dad into *his* arms. He'd been the one to offer the emotional support, all the while knowing that *he* had been the cause. It would have been so easy to return to the Corps, to go back to being a full-time Marine and not have to think about everyone hurting at home. But instead of reenlisting, Cole opted to hang up his dog tags and move back to Montana to help his father rebuild his life. It was what his family needed. What his mother would've wanted. He owed them all at least that much.

"I said come here." It had been a while since he'd heard Phil Dalton issue a command in his no-nonsense, authoritative voice, the one he used to unleash when he was bringing five unruly boys to heel.

And just like a reluctant eight-year-old, Cole hung his head, his feet dragging through the dirt as he stepped into his father's embrace. The older man's arms were still as big and almost as strong as they'd been when Cole was a little boy, and the shoulder he offered now was just as tough and comforting as it had always been.

"It wasn't your fault," his dad whispered as he squeezed his son tighter. "And I'll let you in on a little secret—it wasn't Booker's fault, or Zach's, or Shawn's, or Garrett's, neither. Like I said, every one of us has our own reasons for feeling like we were responsible. But at the end of the day, it was a terrible and tragic accident, and your mama would hate for us to be kicking ourselves over it this way."

Cole shuddered. The weight hadn't exactly been lifted from him, but hearing his father's words, feeling the old man's love wrapped around him, Cole knew that they shared the same burden. And his dad was right. Diana Dalton would never want them beating themselves up over it.

He clung to his father and they stood there like that for a few minutes, not needing any words to express their shared pain. Then a quick honk forced them to take a step back and look at the arriving vehicle.

"We brought out more fencing supplies," Booker said as he climbed from his own truck. "You guys having a party out here or what?"

"Nah," Garrett said as he exited out of the passenger side—after all, nobody was foolish enough to let his lead foot get behind the wheel. "I don't think Cole would throw a party without his personal party planner here to help him."

A bristling sensation made its way down Cole's spine. Garrett had been too hungover the morning after the wedding to ask why he'd been at an apartment complex in Kalispell. And even if his brother had asked, Cole certainly wouldn't have revealed that he'd spent the night with Vivienne. Nor was there any way he would've let it slip that he'd actually hired the woman to plan a fake wedding.

"What are you talking about, Garrett?" Cole asked, praying that his brother didn't *actually* tell them all what he was talking about. He walked to the back of Booker's truck and let down the tailgate.

"That pretty wedding planner? Vivienne?" Garrett grabbed some posts and followed behind Cole. "I heard you two were making out at some pie shop in Kalispell."

"You guys really need to stop getting your gossip from the mailman," Cole grunted as he rolled a huge spool of barbed wire toward his ATV.

"Nah," Garrett said. "I got mine from one of the waitresses at Matilda's. She also works for the caterer who did Zach's reception and she recognized both of you from the wedding."

Booker snickered, dropping another load of posts. "Is that the same waitress you went home with? Or her roommate?"

"Neither." Garrett looked at their dad and at least had the decency to turn an unmanly shade of pink. "Listen. Maybe I had a bit too much to drink that night and was pretty free on who I gave my number to. But we're not talking about me. We're talking about Cole and Vivienne. Should we get the freight house ready for another Dalton wedding?"

*Absolutely not* was the first thing that came to Cole's mind. But he gritted his teeth together before they could accuse him of protesting too much. The supplies had already been emptied from Booker's truck, making it impossible to avoid their curious stares.

"If you boys are so bored that you have time to be standing out here jawing and teasing each other, I'm sure I can find some manure for y'all to haul to the fertilizer plant," their dad suggested, a classic threat from their childhood.

So far, Garrett had been the only kid who'd ever been reckless enough to actually earn that punishment, and judging by his sly grin, he was about to earn it again. "Dad, we don't even have any cattle out here yet."

Booker grabbed their brother by the scruff of his neck. "Don't worry, Pop. I'll get this one back to the barn and find him some muck to shovel up."

The guys threw playful punches at each other, along with some light shoves as they made their way back to the truck. Dust was spitting up from the reversing tires when his dad turned to Cole. "So this wedding planner of yours…"

"She's not exactly *my* wedding planner." Cole hoped a thunderbolt didn't come from the heavens, striking him down for the borderline lie.

"Right. So this Vivienne of yours… You said you don't know what's going on with her right now. Does that mean you're hoping for something more?"

"Dad, since when do you ask us about our love lives?"

"Since I have to do the job of both parents." Phil's words hung in the air and there was no way Cole was going to go back to the emotional subject of his mother's death. He was better off answering his father's question about whether he wanted more with Vivienne.

"Maybe. All I know is that I was doing her a favor, and then it just kinda turned into something else."

Phil lifted a bushy gray eyebrow. "Something else?"

"I don't know, Dad. Yes, I like her, okay? I thought she liked me. But now that the favor is over and she has no need for my help, I haven't heard back from her. Part of me wants to check on her and make sure she's all right because…you know." Again Cole had accidentally circled around to the topic of his mother, and even *he* wasn't so oblivious that he couldn't see he might be overreacting about not hearing from her. "But the other part of me needs to learn to accept that not every unanswered phone call means someone has a problem. Sometimes, it just means that they're over it."

Vivienne hadn't returned Cole's calls right away because she was worried that she might slip and tell him that she'd lost her job. If he found out, there was no doubt he would hop in his truck and floor it all the way to Kalispell wanting to rescue her.

On the other hand, she didn't want to worry him by totally ignoring the messages and letting him think the worst. So on Tuesday afternoon, she sent him a simple text saying she was working on a few things and would call him soon.

It wasn't a complete lie. She *was* working on a few things, namely finding gainful employment. She'd looked at her checking account and, even if she only bought food for Lord Nibbles and limited her grocery-store spending to the bare minimum, she'd barely be able to afford two more months of rent.

Picking up her cell phone and making this call wasn't her first choice. In fact, it felt like an even bigger betrayal to Estelle than the one she'd been accused of. But Vivienne needed a job and it wasn't until she'd lost hers that she realized how much she would miss doing event planning. Sure, she wasn't necessarily any good at bringing in new business; however, she was confident in her abilities to give the clients what they wanted.

While Estelle had promised not to completely pulverize Vivienne's reputation, the woman also hadn't sent over a glowing letter of recommendation with her final paycheck and the personal belongings Vivienne had been forced to leave behind last Friday.

Which put her in a no-win situation.

Since most of the local vendors knew Estelle, they'd start asking questions the minute Vivienne sent out her first résumé. Some of them were familiar enough with her former boss's demanding nature that they might sympathize with Vivienne's less-than-honest approach, but not enough to hire someone they probably wouldn't trust. Nor could she blame them.

When Rich LaRue had left her a message this morning saying he'd heard that not only had Vivienne and her talents been noticeably absent from Valentina Souza's *quinceañera* on Sunday, but she also hadn't been answering calls at Estelle's Events, it reaffirmed her belief that the event-planning grapevine was ripe with juicy gossip about her already.

Watching Lord Nibbles pressed up against the corner of his glass cage—she'd traded out the cheap plastic one he'd come with—Vivienne took comfort in the fact that at least one of them was blissfully unaware and content that their next meal was only a nap away. Her guinea pig was finally overcoming his anxiety issues and she couldn't risk moving him into the apartment she'd dubbed Heartbreak Hotel the first time her dad had shown up asking for a place to stay.

Having no other choice but to see how bad the damage was going to be to her career, she dialed Rich's number and only listened to one full ring before he answered.

"Vivienne!" He didn't attempt to disguise the excitement in his voice. "Is it true? Have you finally told the old dragon that you weren't going to take her crap anymore?"

"Not exactly, Rich." She'd been debating how much she should tell him, but once she began talking, it only felt right to disclose the whole thing. Vivienne told him about her inability to land new clients. She told him about Cole's offer and how she never should have taken it. She even admitted that when she'd run into Rich at the bridal expo, she was there on Estelle's dime while allowing the woman to believe that she was there working. Okay, so, technically, she had been fulfilling part of her duties by doing research and networking. But she'd also been with Cole, which had made the whole trip feel more like a vacation. A reckless and inappropriate vacation that she never wanted to forget.

Rich tsked and made mmm-hmm sounds while she spoke. When Vivienne finished with the part of how Estelle saw them kissing and fired her there on the spot, he gasped and then let out an almost gleeful squeal. "So you're officially a free agent? Estelle can't accuse me of poaching you from her?"

Poaching Vivienne? How could anyone want her after the mess she'd made with Estelle?

"Rich, did you hear what I said? She fired me. And for good reason. She said nobody in town would ever trust me to work for them."

"Darling, do you think you're the first person who had to resort to a bit of trickery to get that she-tiger off their back? Denise over at Perfection Confection once faked an emergency gall bladder surgery rather than admit to Estelle that she couldn't do a wedding cake shaped like a grizzly bear for a couple whose alma mater was UM. Flora, the owner of Flora and Fauna, once told Estelle that red gladiolas were out of season because it was obvious that the bride had her heart set on a white bouquet. She had to hide two buckets full of flowers in the cooler for a month and then sneak them out to the Dumpster in the middle of the night so Estelle wouldn't see that she had them all along. Even Glory, my own sweet wife who is an absolute saint, lied to Estelle about moving to Florida to take care of her dying mother when she quit ten years ago to marry me. Of course, we all know what happened after *that* particular ruse came to light."

"But I lied about Cole being our client," Vivienne pointed out.

"I thought you said he paid her. And signed a contract?"

"He did…"

"Then he was a client," Rich argued. "Look, half the vendors in Kalispell only agree to do business with Estelle if they get a guarantee that they'll only have to work with you."

"So you don't think it will be too hard for me to find a new job?"

"You don't even need to look. I'm hiring you."

Vivienne's breath suspended mid-inhale. She had to remind herself to exhale before asking, "You want me to work for you?"

"I've been trying to get you to come work for me for ages. But here's the thing, Viv. LaVish is expanding and I've already rented out office space in Denver. I have someone for weddings, but I need an employee who could specialize in event planning."

"You mean move to Colorado?" Her mind was spinning.

"Yes. Unless you have something or *someone* keeping you in Montana." His emphasis could only imply that he was talking about Cole.

However, it wasn't like she and Cole were in an actual relationship. Or at least in a relationship that had any sort of potential. He'd agreed eagerly that they were just having fun and keeping things casual.

Growing up, one of the biggest complaints Vivienne would hear from her mother was that Bonnie had given up so many opportunities to be a wife, specifically Richard Shuster's wife. Was Vivienne willing to let an offer like this—which was perfect for her because she'd get to focus on parties, and not get weighed down with all the lovey-dovey romantic details of weddings—pass her by just for some casual fun?

## Chapter Fifteen

"I can't believe Estelle fired you," Lydia said when Vivienne answered her apartment door the following afternoon. "Zach and I just got back from our honeymoon and I went by the office to drop this off. The woman told me she was surprised I would even want to see your face after what you pulled at my wedding."

Lydia held up a gift bag stuffed with tissue. She'd called Vivienne's cell phone a few minutes ago asking if they could meet and Vivienne had invited her over. Though, now that Lydia's eyes were studying the collapsed packing boxes stacked in the corner of her living room, Vivienne wished she had suggested meeting somewhere else.

"Are you moving?"

"I think so."

"You *think* so?" Lydia asked. "Wait. Back up. What does Estelle think you pulled at my wedding? Because as far as I'm concerned, you did an amazing job. I mean, you really went above and beyond."

Well, she had definitely gone above and beyond with the bride's new brother-in-law. Vivienne was suddenly hungry and wanted to ask Lydia to walk to the diner. But this really wasn't a conversation they should have in public. So she went to her small pantry and pulled out a bag of chips. "I don't have any salsa, but I have a nice bottle of chardonnay that Cole and I won at a bridal expo."

"I think I'm going to need a seat for this." Confusion crossed Lydia's face and the newlywed plopped onto the stiff beige sofa. "Cole went with you to a bridal expo?"

In her cupboard, Vivienne found a single wineglass decorated in pink puffy paint with the words *Michelle's Last Stand.* She'd brought it home in a bachelorette party gift bag when one of Michelle's cousins failed to show up for the festivities because she didn't like the fuchsia bridesmaid dress she was being forced to wear. There was some boycotting involved and sides were taken until Vivienne had finally gotten the bride to compromise on having a tailor remove the puffy sleeves.

Vivienne brought the wineglass over to the coffee table, along with a coffee mug bearing the logo of a company that had hired her to throw their corporate holiday party. Hmm. She'd never realized before now how sad it was that she didn't even have a set of matching glasses, let alone a single throw pillow, to pack in those moving boxes.

Handing Lydia the bag of corn chips, Vivienne went to work with the corkscrew. "Cole only went with me because he'd hired me to plan his wedding and we had to go to Billings to get his fiancée's signature for the contract."

Vivienne was glad she hadn't poured any wine yet because Lydia surely would've choked on hers had she taken a drink. "What?" she sputtered.

"Let me start at the beginning," Vivienne offered, then proceeded to come clean to the woman who'd once trusted her. She had to refill Lydia's wine during the telling, but her guest had yet to take a sip of the second glass.

"So, why does Estelle think you pulled something at my wedding?"

"I have no idea. Maybe she thinks that's when I started my affair with Cole."

"Is it?" Lydia asked, then took a hefty drink.

Vivienne didn't want to talk about the intimate details but admitted, "We, uh, had to share a hotel room when we went to Billings, so things had already turned physical before your wedding."

"Okay, but if you and Cole are in a relationship— which I totally approve of, by the way—what's with the moving boxes?" The woman worked for the local paper and really didn't miss a detail.

"I don't think we're in an actual relationship. I mean, we both agreed to keep things casual."

"Is that what you want?"

"I don't know."

"I'm guessing you haven't told him that you've been fired?"

"Are you kidding? If I did, he'd try to fix it. And that's what got us into this mess in the first place."

"You said 'mess.'" Lydia studied her. "If it's supposed to be casual, then how did it get messy?"

"I meant me losing my job. But I guess somewhere along the way, my feelings for him got a little complicated, too."

"Do you love him?"

"I think so. But if he doesn't love me, what's the point in staying?"

Lydia seemed to ponder this a moment before tilting her head. "You know, it's been my experience that the Dalton men don't always know what they want, even if it's right in front of them."

"But I've never been a pusher and love shouldn't have to be forced."

"Does he know you're moving?"

Vivienne bit her lower lip and slowly shook her head. "But I will tell him."

By the time Lydia left, Vivienne was already second-guessing her promise. Especially after she unwrapped the gift, which was a framed picture of Vivienne with Lydia and Zach on their wedding day. No other couple had ever thought to include her when commemorating their big day. She was supposed to stay in the background, to not get emotionally invested.

She knew that it was only right to tell Cole that she was leaving, but she wasn't sure of the best way to say it. The last thing she wanted was to come across as needing him to save her, because that's exactly what he would try to do.

The truth was, Vivienne wanted to be loved, not rescued.

"Just wanted to let you know that I got a job offer in Denver. I can never tell you how much you meant to… how much it meant that you helped me out with Estelle. Anyway, I wanted to thank you and wish you the best."

Her voice sounded upbeat at first, but then there had been a slight catch. Or maybe Cole was imagining it. He listened to Vivienne's message for the third time. Though, now he was far enough away from the sawing and hammering and loud voices of his brothers working inside the stables.

She was moving to Colorado? Out of the blue like that?

Why?

And why had she called to tell him? Especially when the last time they'd texted, she'd said she was very busy and he hadn't heard from her since. He wanted to convince himself that with her leaving like this, he was going to be better off. He was going to be able to get through a day of work without thinking about her a hundred times and worrying when it would all end for the two of them. Unfortunately, his confusion at her message and the timing of it didn't help to persuade him of the positives.

"Was that the pretty wedding planner?" his dad asked, surprising Cole by coming out of the stables.

"Yeah," Cole replied, still replaying her words in his mind.

"Are you going to see her soon?"

"I, uh, guess not. Sounds like she's moving to Colorado for a new job."

"Really? That's a surprise. You'd think she'd have all the work she could handle right here in Rust Creek alone."

"You'd think," Cole echoed, disappointment clawing at him.

"So you're not going to see her before she goes?"

"I guess not."

"Hmm..." his dad said, and Cole jerked his head up.

"What's that?"

"I was just mumbling."

"No, you weren't. You said 'hmm,'" Cole accused. "The way you do whenever you're trying to get one of us to do something we don't want to do."

"So you're saying that you *don't* want to see her before she goes?"

"I didn't say that."

"Heck, Cole, you're blaming me for trying to get you to do something you don't want to do. All I want here is to figure out what exactly that is."

"Okay, so maybe I *do* want to see her. But maybe I also know I dodged a painful bullet later on down the road."

"Since when do you dodge bullets?"

"Since I found out that loving someone hurts."

"Of course it hurts, son. It's also what makes the pain worth it. I've seen the way you look at Vivienne.

It's the same way I used to look at your mama. I'm not such an old man that I don't recognize that look in my own sons." His father held up a palm when Cole began to respond. "Now, before you start on all that 'losing somebody doesn't make it worth the risk' nonsense, let me stop you right there. For thirty-five years, I loved your mother, okay? In fact, I loved that woman so dang much it tore me up inside when I lost her. But I'll tell you this much. I'd happily go through every single second of that grief all over again, even if I only got to love her for half as long."

## Chapter Sixteen

After Lydia had left her apartment, Vivienne succumbed to a moment of weakness and went out to her car to retrieve the planning binder she'd purposely stashed in her trunk after the fateful afternoon when Estelle had fired her. She hadn't wanted any reminders of Cole to influence her decision about taking the job with A LaVish Affair.

That same night, though, she'd poured herself another glass of wine and opened the binder before staring at the pictures Cole had cut out from magazines or printed off the internet. None of the pictures had a single wedding detail in them. They were all of tropical beach destinations and shoved into the folder marked Honeymoon Ideas.

The man truly had no desire to get married and it

was suddenly clear that Vivienne needed to let him go and move on with her life. The following morning, she'd waited until she knew he'd be busy working at the ranch and called him, a calming relief settling over her when his voice mail picked up.

It had been three full days since Vivienne had left Cole that message about her leaving town. When he didn't respond, Vivienne had the bittersweet satisfaction of being right all along. The guy had never been looking for something serious in the first place. And since she'd been very careful in not mentioning anything about being fired, it proved her theory that he only came running when he thought she'd issued an SOS.

There was nothing left for her in Kalispell.

"I think you'll like Denver," she told Lord Nibbles as he rolled through the living room, exploring the apartment in his clear plastic exercise ball. When Vivienne began taping moving boxes together, the guinea pig had gotten restless in his cage, pacing back and forth and twitching his nose at lightning speed. She was determined to keep his anxiety about the upcoming move at a minimum, so she'd put him in his ball to allow him to expend some energy.

Now if she could only convince herself that everything was working out for the best. Standing in her kitchen, she opened a cupboard and, for the millionth time that week, stared at the hodgepodge of contents inside and debated whether or not she should even bother taking the mismatched glasses and plates with her.

She was starting a new job in a new state. Maybe it was time to buy herself a proper set of kitchenware for her new home. Rich had promised to increase her salary; however, she was still going to be on a tight budget for the first few months.

The knock on her door startled her out of her inner debate about needing more than a four-piece set of silverware and she almost tripped over Lord Nibbles as he ran in his ball toward the bedroom to get away from the unfamiliar sound.

Since Vivienne wasn't expecting anyone, she looked through the peephole, then flattened her forehead against the wood panel of the door, squeezing her eyes shut and only reopening one to take another peek. To make sure that her mind wasn't playing tricks on her.

Yep. That was Cole Dalton, all right. Standing on the tiny concrete stoop in front of her apartment, his cowboy hat firmly in place and his plaid sleeves rolled up on his forearms, as though he was about to get to work.

Maybe he was here to offer his expert packing services.

She took three deep breaths before finally unlatching the dead bolt and twisting open the knob. "Hey."

"Hi, there." He took off his hat and Vivienne's stomach dropped. Why did he have to be so handsome and charming? She leaned against the edge of the door for support, then realized she wasn't being very hospitable when he drawled, "May I come in?"

"Of course." She stepped back. "But watch out for Lord Nibbles. He's on a tear racing around this place in his exercise ball."

If her heart hadn't been falling apart at the sight of him, it would've been comical to watch Cole in his boots, carefully scanning the carpet and taking small steps to ensure he didn't accidentally kick her guinea pig.

"So you're really moving?" He jerked his chin toward the still-empty moving boxes lined up on her sofa.

"It's looking that way," she said, then clamped her jaw shut. No, it wasn't *looking* that way. It *was* that way. She was moving. Why couldn't she just come out and say it?

"That's too bad." His words were like a jump start to her heart and her pulse began pounding.

"Why's that?"

"Because I need to hire a wedding planner."

This again? Her shoulders dropped in defeat. "Unfortunately, I'm no longer in that line of work."

"You mean you're not moving for another wedding-planner job?"

"Technically, Rich is hiring me as an events planner. But I can refer you to Estelle's Events for all your wedding-planning needs."

"I don't want Estelle. I want you."

Vivienne looked up at her ceiling, trying to get her fluttering emotions in check. "Is it me you want or is it just another chance at rescuing me that brought you here?"

He stepped closer to her. "I want *you*."

"I thought you wanted to keep things casual."

"I thought that was what I wanted, too." His fingers swept along her jaw. "But then something changed."

"What if something changes again?" she asked, refusing to let her racing heart take over her rational head. "I don't want to be like my parents—in and out of love over and over again."

"I'm a Dalton." He slowly winked and her tense muscles went soft. "Once we fall in love, we're as good as gone. I can't help it."

She flattened her palms against his chest, but she didn't push him away. "What about marriage?"

"Are you proposing to me?"

"No. Not now," she said, and he raised an eyebrow. "I mean, we both made an awful lot of fun of the institution of marriage. But what if down the road one of us…" She trailed off.

"I never made fun of the institution of marriage. I made fun of weddings. Didn't you look at my binder? It was full of places where we could elope." He rested his hand on her waist. "I love you, Vivienne."

Her throat tightened, and all she could do was look at him.

His dad had said that loving someone was worth the risk of losing them. But when Cole finally admitted his love, she didn't reply. She just stood there, searching his face for something, but he had no idea what.

"Can you please say something?"

"You love me?" she asked, her voice barely louder than a whisper.

"How could I not? You're selfless and creative and smart and beautiful, and being with you always feels right."

"So you're not here to rescue me?"

"What would I need to rescue you from?"

"Estelle fired me."

Anger surged through him, making his skin tight

and his feet restless. Yet he wasn't able to release her. "Why in the world would she fire you? You're the best wedding planner in all of Montana. And trust me, I've been to the biggest wedding expo in the state, so I'm officially a reluctant expert on this subject."

"She saw us kissing last week after we met for lunch."

"So? You're not allowed to date a client?"

"Not an *engaged* client."

Realization sank in. She'd lost her job because of him. Pieces of the puzzle fell into place, and now he understood why she hadn't been quick to return his calls and texts. "Why didn't you tell me?"

"Because I was afraid you would drive over to Estelle's and tell her the truth and demand that she take me back."

"That's exactly what I would've done."

Vivienne's palms slid up his chest and toward his cheeks, holding his head in place. "I didn't want you to rescue me. I'd been unhappy working for her for a long time and I needed to rescue myself."

Her smooth hands felt so good on his skin he didn't want to shift his head. He caught a glimpse of the cardboard boxes out of the corner of his eye. "So that's why you took the job in Denver."

"I thought you wanted to keep things casual," she said, and his gut twisted, hoping she wasn't about to shoot him down. "There was nothing else for me here but heartbreak."

He clung to that last word. "I never want to break your heart."

"You can't save me all the time, Cole." Her warning whispered against his skin as she pulled his face closer.

"I know. When I came up with the idea of hiring you, I thought I was coming to your aid. But somewhere along the way, you ended up rescuing me."

Her lashes fluttered closed and a soft smile spread across her face. "I think I fell in love with you that day inside your cousin's pink bathroom."

Warmth flooded Cole, filling him with both relief and passion, and he closed the space between their lips. As he kissed her hungrily, all he could think was that this woman in his arms loved him. He would do everything in his power to keep her happy.

"Tell me again," he said.

"I love you, Cole Dalton." Vivienne traced a finger along his lower lip just as something crashed into his ankle and he looked down to see the little black-and-white guinea pig in its plastic ball.

It brought Cole back to the present situation and Vivienne's upcoming job. If they were going to make this a successful relationship, he couldn't be rushing in and fixing things for her all the time. "Listen, I don't want to stand between you and your career, but do you think we could do that whole eloping thing before we move to Colorado?"

"We?" Her eyes widened. "You'd move with me? What about helping your dad on the ranch?"

"I have four other brothers. It's time for one of them to take on the hero role for a change."

Vivienne chuckled, then grew serious. "Cole, I would never ask you to leave your family. They mean more to you than any job ever will to me. Besides, if what you say about all you Daltons falling in love is true, there are going to be plenty of upcoming weddings and baby showers to plan in Rust Creek Falls."

For the first time in his life, Cole didn't need a plan; he didn't need to make a decision right this second. All he needed was Vivienne.

# *Epilogue*

Nobody was more surprised than Vivienne when Estelle called her the following morning. At first, she assumed her former boss had heard about her job offer with A LaVish Affair and was calling to threaten to have her blackballed all the way down in Colorado. But the woman's voice was unusually raspy and even cordial when she announced her reason for the call. "Viv, I'd like you to buy me out."

"I beg your pardon?" Vivienne asked, pulling the bedsheet off Cole so she could cover her own nudity as she sat up.

"My doctor has been after me to retire for years and relocate to a warmer locale. I've been fighting it, but after you left, I realized that I just can't keep up like I used to."

"I'm sorry to hear that, Estelle, but I think your doctor is probably right."

"Meh. We'll see. I've got a sister in Phoenix who owns a funeral home and she said business never slows down over there. So I'll still want to take some event-planning binders with me, but maybe we can work out a deal for the rest of the office supplies."

Vivienne shuddered at the funeral-type events Estelle was hoping to plan. But she wished the woman well and agreed to meet with an attorney to go over the details. Really, there wasn't much to buy, since Vivienne could've easily just started her own company and taken over any outstanding clients and vendor contracts. But Estelle had given her a start in the business, and she didn't feel right not giving the woman some sort of fair compensation.

She also called Rich LaRue and told him she wasn't going to be able to take the job offer after all, since she would be moving to Rust Creek Falls once their wing in the main house was built on the Dalton property. The man was gracious and offered to give her the friends and family rate if she wanted him to plan her wedding.

"That's very kind of you, Rich, but Cole and I are planning to elope."

His gasp was sharp and a bit melodramatic. "Don't ever let me hear you use that word again, young lady."

Elopements were the bane to a wedding planner's business and it was an industry custom to never speak of them. She rolled her eyes as she attempted to placate him. "I know, but Cole and I both will have so much going on with me launching a new business and his family starting up their ranch."

That much was true. It ended up taking several months to get the main house built, and with Vivienne working at the office in Kalispell and Cole putting in long hours herding cattle at the ranch, they decided that once the lease was up, Vivienne would move everyday operations to the renovated train depot at Sawmill Station. And with all the referrals coming her way from his extended family and all their friends, Vivienne had to hire her own Junior Wedding Planner to cover for her while she and Cole finally got to have the destination wedding of their dreams.

Vivienne wore a simple white linen shift and a crown of wild orchids in her loose hair as she walked across a sandy white beach in Bora-Bora. Cole was standing on the water's edge, barefoot with his jeans rolled up to his calves, his casual white shirt unbuttoned at the neck and his favorite straw cowboy hat keeping the setting sun out of his eyes.

She'd once told him that every bride and groom wanted their wedding day to be a fairy tale. And on this day, she and Cole Dalton were finally getting their happily-ever-after.

\* \* \* \* \*

*Love those Montana Mavericks?*

*They'll be riding back into town next month
in the new Special Edition continuity*

**MONTANA MAVERICKS:
THE LONELYHEARTS RANCH**

*Coming July 2018,
wherever Harlequin books and ebooks are sold.*

*Once, in secret, Derek Dalton and Amy Wainwright
said "I do." Reunited a decade later
for their best friends' wedding,
can the love they lost be found again?*

*Don't miss*

*A MAVERICK TO (RE)MARRY
By New York Times bestselling author
Christine Rimmer*

*THE MAVERICK'S BABY-IN-WAITING
By Melissa Senate
On sale August 2018.*

*And if you loved this book by Christy Jeffries,
look for
A PROPOSAL FOR THE OFFICER
Available now!*

*Keep reading for a special preview of*
*HERONS LANDING,*
*the first in an exciting new series from*
New York Times *bestselling author*
*JoAnn Ross and HQN Books!*

# CHAPTER ONE

SETH HARPER WAS spending a Sunday spring afternoon detailing his wife's Rallye Red Honda Civic when he learned that she'd been killed by a suicide bomber in Afghanistan.

Despite the Pacific Northwest's reputation for unrelenting rain, the sun was shining so brightly that the Army notification officers—a man and a woman in dark blue uniforms and black shoes spit-shined to a mirror gloss—had been wearing shades. Or maybe, Seth considered, as they'd approached the driveway in what appeared to be slow motion, they would've worn them anyway. Like armor, providing emotional distance from the poor bastard whose life they were about to blow to smithereens.

At the one survivor grief meeting he'd later attended

(only to get his fretting mother off his back), he'd heard stories from other spouses who'd experienced a sudden, painful jolt of loss before their official notice. Seth hadn't received any advance warning. Which was why, at first, the officers' words had been an incomprehensible buzz in his ears. Like distant radio static.

Zoe couldn't be dead. His wife wasn't a combat soldier. She was an Army surgical nurse, working in a heavily protected military base hospital, who'd be returning to civilian life in two weeks. Seth still had a bunch of stuff on his homecoming punch list to do. After buffing the wax off the Civic's hood and shining up the chrome wheels, his next project was to paint the walls white in the nursery he'd added on to their Folk Victorian cottage for the baby they'd be making.

She'd begun talking a lot about baby stuff early in her deployment. Although Seth was as clueless as the average guy about a woman's mind, it didn't take Dr. Phil to realize that she was using the plan to start a family as a touchstone. Something to hang on to during their separation.

In hours of Skype calls between Honeymoon Harbor and Kabul, they'd discussed the pros and cons of the various names on a list that had grown longer each time they'd talked. While the names remained up in the air, she *had* decided that whatever their baby's gender, the nursery should be a bright white to counter the Olympic Peninsula's gray skies.

She'd also sent him links that he'd dutifully followed to Pinterest pages showing bright crib bedding, mobiles and wooden name letters in primary crayon shades of blue, green, yellow and red. Even as Seth had lobbied for Seattle Seahawk navy and action green, he'd known that he'd end up giving his wife whatever she wanted.

The same as he'd been doing since the day he fell head over heels in love with her back in middle school.

Meanwhile, planning to get started on that baby making as soon as she got back to Honeymoon Harbor, he'd built the nursery as a welcome-home surprise.

Then Zoe had arrived at Sea-Tac airport in a flag-draped casket.

And two years after the worst day of his life, the room remained unpainted behind a closed door Seth had never opened since.

MANNION'S PUB & BREWERY was located on the street floor of a faded redbrick building next to Honeymoon Harbor's ferry landing. The former salmon cannery had been one of many buildings constructed after the devastating 1893 fire that had swept along the waterfront, burning down the original wood buildings. One of Seth's ancestors, Jacob Harper, had built the replacement in 1894 for the town's mayor and pub owner, Finn Mannion. Despite the inability of Washington authorities to keep Canadian alcohol from flooding into the state, the pub had been shuttered during Prohibition in the 1930s, effectively putting the Mannions out of the pub business until Quinn Mannion had returned home from Seattle and hired Harper Construction to reclaim the abandoned space.

Although the old Victorian seaport town wouldn't swing into full tourist mode until Memorial Day, nearly every table was filled when Seth dropped in at the end of the day. He'd no sooner slid onto a stool at the end of the long wooden bar when Quinn, who'd been washing glasses in a sink, stuck a bottle of Shipwreck CDA in front of him.

"Double cheddar bacon or stuffed blue cheese?" he asked.

"Double cheddar bacon." As he answered the question, it crossed Seth's mind that his life—what little he had outside his work of restoring the town's Victorian buildings constructed by an earlier generation of Harpers—had possibly slid downhill beyond routine to boringly predictable. "And don't bother boxing it up. I'll be eating it here," he added.

Quinn lifted a dark brow. "I didn't see that coming."

Meaning that, by having dinner here at the pub six nights a week, the seventh being with Zoe's parents—where they'd recount old memories, and look through scrapbooks of photos that continued to cause an ache deep in his heart—he'd undoubtedly landed in the predictable zone. So, what was wrong with that? Predictability was an underrated concept. By definition, it meant a lack of out-of-the-blue surprises that might destroy life as you knew it. Some people might like change. Seth was not one of them. Which was why he always ordered takeout with his first beer of the night.

The second beer he drank at home with his burger and fries. While other guys in his position might have escaped reality by hitting the bottle, Seth always stuck to a limit of two bottles, beginning with that long, lonely dark night after burying his wife. Because, although hc'd never had a problem with alcohol, he harbored a secret fear that if he gave in to the temptation to begin seriously drinking, he might never stop.

The same way if he ever gave in to the anger, the unfairness of what the hell had happened, he'd have to patch a lot more walls in his house than he had those first few months after the notification officers' arrival.

There'd been times when he'd decided that someone in the Army had made a mistake. That Zoe hadn't died at all. Maybe she'd been captured during a melee and no one knew enough to go out searching for her. Or perhaps she was lying in some other hospital bed, her face all bandaged, maybe with amnesia, or even in a coma, and some lab tech had mixed up blood samples with another soldier who'd died. That could happen, right?

But as days slid into weeks, then weeks into months, he'd come to accept that his wife really was gone. Most of the time. Except when he'd see her, from behind, strolling down the street, window-shopping or walking onto the ferry, her dark curls blowing into a frothy tangle. He'd embarrassed himself a couple times by calling out her name. Now he never saw her at all. And worse yet, less and less in his memory. Zoe was fading away. Like that ghost who reputedly haunted Herons Landing, the old Victorian mansion up on the bluff overlooking the harbor.

"I'm having dinner with Mom tonight." And had been dreading it all the damn day. Fortunately, his dad hadn't heard about it yet. But since news traveled at the speed of sound in Honeymoon Harbor, he undoubtedly soon would.

"You sure you don't want to wait to order until she gets here?"

"She's not eating here. It's a command-performance dinner," he said. "To have dinner with her and the guy who may be her new boyfriend. Instead of eating at her new apartment, she decided that it'd be better to meet on neutral ground."

"Meaning somewhere other than a brewpub owned and operated by a Mannion," Quinn said. "Especially given the rumors that said new boyfriend just happens to be my uncle Mike."

"That does make the situation stickier." Seth took a long pull on the Cascadian Dark Ale and wished it was something stronger.

The feud between the Harpers and Mannions dated back to the early 1900s. After having experienced a boom during the end of the nineteenth century, the once-bustling seaport town had fallen on hard times during a national financial depression.

Although the population declined drastically, those dreamers who'd remained were handed a stroke of luck in 1910 when the newlywed king and queen of Montacroix added the town to their honeymoon tour of America. The couple had learned of this lush green region from the king's friend Theodore Roosevelt, who'd set aside national land for the Mount Olympus Monument.

As a way of honoring the royals, and hoping that the national and European press following them across the country might bring more attention to the town, residents had voted nearly unanimously to change the name to Honeymoon Harbor. Seth's ancestor Nathaniel

Harper had been the lone holdout, creating acrimony on both sides that continued to linger among some but not all of the citizens. Quinn's father, after all, was a Mannion, his mother a Harper. But Ben Harper, Seth's father, tended to nurse his grudges. Even century-old ones that had nothing to do with him. Or at least hadn't. Until lately.

"And it gets worse," he said.

"Okay."

One of the things that made Quinn such a good bartender was that he listened a lot more than he talked. Which made Seth wonder how he'd managed to spend all those years as a big-bucks corporate lawyer in Seattle before returning home to open this pub and microbrewery.

"The neutral location she chose is Leaf."

Quinn's quick laugh caused two women who were drinking wine at a table looking out over the water to glance up with interest. Which wasn't surprising. Quinn's brother Wall Street wizard Gabe Mannion might be richer, New York City pro quarterback Burke Mannion flashier, and, last time he'd seen him, which had admittedly been a while, Marine-turned-LA-cop Aiden Mannion had still carried that bad-boy vibe that had gotten him in trouble a lot while they'd been growing up together. But Quinn's superpower had always been the ability to draw the attention of females—from bald babies in strollers to blue-haired elderly women in walkers—without seeming to do a thing.

After turning in the burger order, and helping out his

waitress by delivering meals to two of the tables, Quinn returned to the bar and began hanging up the glasses.

"Let me guess," he said. "You ordered the burger as an appetizer before you go off to a vegetarian restaurant to dine on alfalfa sprouts and pretty flowers."

"It's a matter of survival. I spent the entire day until I walked in here taking down a wall, adding a new reinforcing beam and framing out a bathroom. A guy needs sustenance. Not a plate of arugula and pansies."

"Since I run a place that specializes in pub grub, you're not going to get any argument from me on that plan. Do you still want the burger to go for the mutt?"

Bandit, a black Lab/boxer mix so named for his penchant for stealing food from Seth's construction sites back in his stray days—including once gnawing through a canvas ice chest—usually waited patiently in the truck for his burger. Tonight Seth had dropped him off at the house on his way over here, meaning the dog would have to wait a little longer for his dinner. Not that he hadn't mooched enough from the framers already today. If the vet hadn't explained strays' tendencies for overeating because they didn't know where their next meal might be coming from, Seth might have suspected the street-scarred dog he'd rescued of having a tapeworm.

They shot the breeze while Quinn served up drinks, which in this place ran more to the craft beer he brewed in the building next door. A few minutes later, the swinging door to the kitchen opened and out came two layers of prime beef topped with melted local cheddar cheese, bacon and caramelized grilled onions, with a slice of tomato and an iceberg-lettuce leaf tossed in as an apparent nod to the food pyramid, all piled between the halves of an oversize toasted kaiser bun. Taking up the rest of the heated metal platter was a mountain of spicy French fries.

Next to the platter was a take-out box of plain burger. It wouldn't stay warm, but having first seen the dog scrounging from a garbage can on the waterfront, Seth figured Bandit didn't care about the temperature of his dinner.

"So, you're eating in tonight," a bearded giant wearing a T-shirt with Embrace the Lard on the front said in a deep foghorn voice. "I didn't see that coming."

"Everyone's a damn joker," Seth muttered, even as the aroma of grilled beef and melted cheese drew him in. He took a bite and nearly moaned. The Norwegian, who'd given up cooking on fishing boats when he'd gotten tired of freezing his ass off during winter crabbing season, might be a sarcastic smart-ass, but the guy sure as hell could cook.

"He's got a dinner date tonight at Leaf." Quinn, for some damn reason, chose this moment to decide to get chatty. "This is an appetizer."

Jarle Bjornstad snorted. "I tried going vegan," he said. "I'd hooked up with a woman in Anchorage who wouldn't even wear leather. It didn't work out."

"Mine's not that kind of date." Seth wondered how much arugula, kale and flowers it would take to fill up the man with shoulders as wide as a redwood trunk and arms like huge steel bands. His full-sleeve tattoo boasted a butcher's chart of a cow. Which might explain his ability to turn a beef patty into something close to nirvana. "And there probably aren't enough vegetables on the planet to sustain you."

During the remodeling, Seth had taken out four rows of bricks in the wall leading to the kitchen to allow the six-foot-seven-inch-tall cook to go back and forth without having to duck his head to keep from hitting the doorjamb every trip.

"On our first date, she cited all this damn research claiming vegans lived nine years longer than meat eaters." Jarle's teeth flashed in a grin in his flaming red beard. "After a week of grazing, I decided that her statistics might be true, but that extra time would be nine horrible baconless years."

That said, he turned and stomped back into the kitchen.

"He's got a point," Quinn said.

"Amen to that." Having learned firsthand how treacherous and unpredictable death could be, with his current family situation on the verge of possibly exploding, Seth decided to worry about his arteries later and took another huge bite of beef-and-cheese heaven.

*Need to know what happens next?*
*Order your copy of HERONS LANDING*
*wherever you buy your books!*

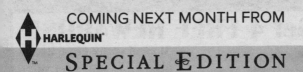

# COMING NEXT MONTH FROM
# HARLEQUIN
# SPECIAL EDITION

## Available June 19, 2018

### #2629 A MAVERICK TO (RE)MARRY
*Montana Mavericks: The Lonelyhearts Ranch* • by Christine Rimmer
Not only were Derek Dalton and Amy Wainwright once an item, they were actually married! With Amy back in town for her friend's wedding, how long before their secret past is revealed?

### #2630 DETECTIVE BARELLI'S LEGENDARY TRIPLETS
*The Wyoming Multiples* • by Melissa Senate
Norah Ingalls went to bed a single mom of triplets—and woke up married! They might try to blame it on the spiked punch, but Detective Reed Barelli is finding it impossible to walk away from this instant family!

### #2631 HOW TO ROMANCE A RUNAWAY BRIDE
*Wilde Hearts* • by Teri Wilson
Days before she turns thirty, Allegra Clark finds herself a runaway bride! Lucky for her, she accidentally crashes a birthday party for Zander Wilde—the man who promised to marry her if neither of them was married by thirty...

### #2632 THE SOLDIER'S TWIN SURPRISE
*Rocking Chair Rodeo* • by Judy Duarte
Erica Campbell is only here to give army pilot Clay Matthews the news: she's having his babies. Two of them! But can she count on Clay—a man whose dreams of military glory have just been dashed—to be her partner in parenthood?

### #2633 THE SECRET SON'S HOMECOMING
*The Cedar River Cowboys* • by Helen Lacey
Jonah Rickard, the illegitimate son of J. D. O'Sullivan, wants nothing to do with his "other" family. Unfortunately, he's falling for Connie Bedford, who's practically part of the family, and he'll have to confront his past to claim the future he wants.

### #2634 THE CAPTAIN'S BABY BARGAIN
*American Heroes* • by Merline Lovelace
After one hot night, Captain Suzanne Hall remembers everything she craved about her sexy ex-husband. Now she's pregnant and Gabe thinks they should get married...again! Will they be able to overcome everything that tore them apart before?

---

*Is that what you want?* The question was still there, in his
eyes. All she had to do was decide.

She took a deep breath and shook her head.

Zander leaned closer, his eyes hard on hers. Then he
reached to cup her face with his free hand and drew the
pad of his thumb slowly, deliberately along the swell of
her bottom lip. "Tell me what you want, Allegra."

*You.* She swallowed. *I want you.*

"This," she said, reaching up on tiptoe to close the
space between them and touch her lips to his.

*What are you doing? Stop.*

But it was too late to change her mind. Too late to
pretend she didn't want this. Because the moment her
mouth grazed Zander's, he took ownership of the kiss.

His hands slid into her hair, holding her in place, while
his tongue slid brazenly along the seam of her lips until
they parted, opening for him.

Then there was nothing but heat and want and the
shocking reality that this was what she'd wanted all
along. Zander.

HSEEXP0618

Had she always felt this way? It seemed impossible. Yet beneath the newness of his mouth on hers and the crush of her breasts against the solid wall of his chest, there was something else. A feeling she couldn't quite put her finger on. A sense of belonging. Of destiny.

Home.

Allegra squeezed her eyes closed. She didn't want to imagine herself fitting into this life again. There was too much at stake. Too much to lose. But no matter how hard she railed against it, there it was, shimmering before like her a mirage.

She whimpered into Zander's mouth, and he groaned in return, gently guiding her backward until her spine was pressed against the cool marble wall. Before she could register what was happening, he gathered her wrists and pinned them above her head with a single, capable hand. And the last remaining traces of resistance melted away. She couldn't fight it anymore. Not from this position of delicious surrender. Her arms went lax, and somewhere in the back of her mind, a wall came tumbling down.

The breath rushed from her body, and a memory came into focus with perfect, crystalline clarity.

*Let's make a deal. If neither of us is married by the time we turn thirty, we'll marry each other. Agreed?*

*Agreed?*

*Don't miss*
*HOW TO ROMANCE A RUNAWAY BRIDE*
*by Teri Wilson, available July 2018 wherever*
*Harlequin® Special Edition books and ebooks are sold.*

www.Harlequin.com

# THE WORLD IS BETTER WITH

## WITH

# Romance

Harlequin has everything from contemporary, passionate and heartwarming to suspenseful and inspirational stories.

Whatever your mood,
we have a romance just for you!

Connect with us to find your next great read, special offers and more.

f /HarlequinBooks

🐦 @HarlequinBooks

www.HarlequinBlog.com

www.Harlequin.com/Newsletters

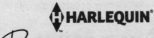

## ⊞ HARLEQUIN®

A *Romance* FOR EVERY MOOD™

www.Harlequin.com

*LOVE*
# Harlequin
# romance?

Join our Harlequin community to share your thoughts and connect with other romance readers!

Be the first to find out about promotions, news, and exclusive content!

Sign up for the Harlequin e-newsletter and download a free book from any series at

## www.TryHarlequin.com

---

**CONNECT WITH US AT:**

Harlequin.com/Community

 Facebook.com/HarlequinBooks

 Twitter.com/HarlequinBooks

 Instagram.com/HarlequinBooks

 Pinterest.com/HarlequinBooks

ReaderService.com

 **HARLEQUIN®**

**ROMANCE WHEN
YOU NEED IT**